W9-CTE-176

Contents

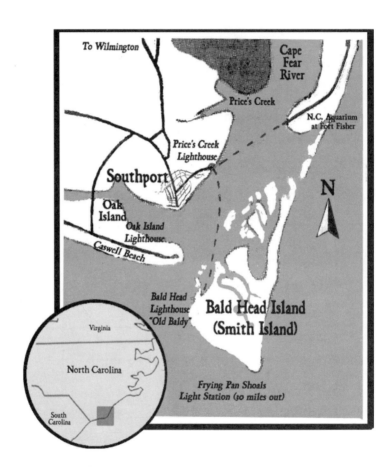

Cape Fear, NC

Do You Have a Minute?

"Nothing could be finer
than to be in Carolina in the morning."

Gus Kahn, "Carolina in the Morning" 1922. Music by Walter Donaldson

I grew up in North Carolina, so the North Carolina lighthouses and I have been friends for a long time.

I was born in the middle part of the state—in the high point of the section between the mountains and the coastal plain that they call the piedmont—but almost every year my family traveled east to the beach for part of our summer vacation.

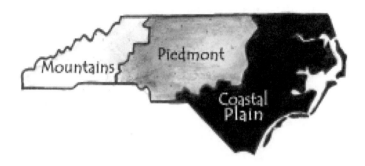

After I moved away from home to California, I didn't get back to the North Carolina beaches much—actually not at all. I went to some amazingly beautiful beaches in Northern California, but they were different from the North Carolina beaches.

You see, while the Northern California beaches are rocky with crashing waves and ice cold water, the beaches on the North Carolina coast are flat and sandy, and the water is warm. When you walk on the beach in North Carolina, you can go on and on and on almost forever. It's pretty amazing.

The year after my twin nieces were born, my family in North Carolina decided we needed a place for all of us to get together during the summer. We rented a house right on the beach, and every summer since then—for the past 25 years—our family has gathered for a week on North Carolina's Oak Island.

The times I've spent on Oak Island have been a special part of my life in many different ways. I hope that these North Carolina lighthouse adventures will let you experience some of the magic I've enjoyed there over the years.

Don't Skip the Hard Words

Most of the time when you're reading and don't know a word, you can figure out what it means from the other words or phrases around it. (That's called **context**.)

context (KAHN-tekst) The words or sentences around a word that help explain its meaning.

But sometimes the context isn't there. Does that mean you should skip the word? I hope you don't!

In this book, I've added some definitions to help with words you might not know. So, if you're reading and see a word in a paragraph that's in bold letters (like the word "context" on the previous page), you should look around for a definition of that word. The definition will help you understand the story better and may even help you add some new words to your vocabulary!

Fact or Fiction?

You probably know that Sam and Becky and their friends and family are not real people. This is, after all, a fictional story and all the characters are made up. But the places I describe and the historical people and events that I tell you about are very real.

In fact, there's one more thing you should know about the North Carolina coast—

something that has always fascinated me about the North Carolina beaches.

In some places along the coast, when the **tide** is low you can walk straight out into the ocean on the sandbars for a long, long, *long* way and still be only waist-deep in water.

The shallow water is fun for those of us who like to play in the waves, but for ships sailing along the North Carolina coast, the shallow waters were—and still are— extremely dangerous.

tide

(TIED)
The daily rising and falling of the water level because of the moon's gravity pulling on the earth's oceans.

Every day at the beach there is a high tide, a low tide, another high tide, and another low tide—about 6 hours apart. the continuous rising and falling of the water level causes the waves at the beach.

It's no **coincidence** that the little point of land that sticks out into the Atlantic Ocean near Oak Island is called Cape Fear, and it's no coincidence that the waters

coincidence

(CO-IN-seh-dense)
Things that seem to have a connection, but are really only related by accident.

along the North Carolina coast are known to sailors all over the world as the "Graveyard of the Atlantic."

Read More

There are many wonderful books and web sites about lighthouses in general and about North Carolina lighthouses in particular. I've  included a list of some of my favorites for you at the end of this book.

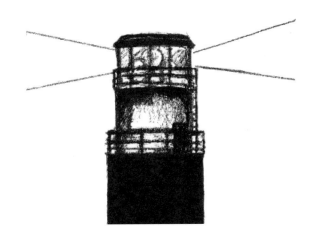

Chapter 1
Too Short

One-two-three-four-off. One-two-three-four-off. One-two-three-four-off.

"If *I* were a lighthouse," said Troy, mostly to himself, "I don't think I'd want to flash the same flash all the time. I mean, how dull is that?"

"You *have* to flash the same signal every time. That's what lighthouses do." Troy's twin brother, Andrew, was lying on his stomach on the bottom bunk, reading… as usual. His new favorite book was about pirates, and he didn't even look up as he answered Troy.

"If I were a lighthouse," Troy said, "I'd flash my light any way I felt like it."

"Then you wouldn't be a very *good* lighthouse," said Andrew. "Each lighthouse has a different flash pattern so the sailors can figure out where they are."

"So, you mean when they see a one-two-three-four-off flash they know they're here?"

"Exactly."

"No way. What about radar and sonar and satellites and all the other things that help you know where you are? I mean, don't they use that global positioning stuff—you know, GPS?"

"It's global positioning *system*, not global positioning stuff, and yes, they do use all that," said Andrew as he slowly turned a page.

"But most lighthouses were built before ships had all that. Sailors used maps and charts to figure out where they were, but they also needed the lighthouses—especially in a storm. When the captain of a ship saw a lighthouse that flashed one-two-three-four-off, he knew it was the Oak Island Lighthouse."

Andrew turned to the next page. "Besides, you might not have time to look at your GPS

if you were being chased by pirates. If they caught you, they'd throw you overboard and steal your gold."

"I still think it's boring," muttered Troy. He was lying on his back, on the top bunk, in the third bedroom of the beachfront house that his parents had rented on North Carolina's Oak Island. The side window in the boys' room looked right at the Oak Island Lighthouse, which flashed the same pattern all day and all night.

"One-two-three-four-off. One-two-three-four-off. Maybe it changes when nobody's watching. What do you think, Andrew? Andrew?"

But Andrew was too busy reading about pirates—specifically about a pirate named Blackbeard.

Troy sighed. Maybe he should get one of Andrew's books to read. Anything was better than watching that dumb lighthouse flash the same dumb pattern.

One-two-three-four-off. One-two-three-off…Wait, what?

That's weird, thought Troy. I must have miscounted. He waited and counted again.

One-two-three-four-off. That was right.

One-two-three-off. Three flashes! Not the four flashes that were supposed to be there. Troy counted again.

One-two-three-four-off. One-two-three-four-off. One-two-three-off! Could a lighthouse change its flash?

1,2,3,4...OFF...
1,2,3,4...OFF...
1,2,3, ... OFF...
WHAT ???

"Andrew, did you see that?"

"See what?" mumbled Andrew, his face close to his book.

"The lighthouse! It only flashed three times—it's supposed to have four."

"Very funny, Troy. Can't you just go to sleep and let me read?"

"I'm not kidding, Andrew! I promise! The lighthouse only flashed three flashes!"

"You just miscounted. A lighthouse doesn't change its flashes. It's on a computer, and there's no way to change it unless you reprogram the computer." Andrew looked up from his book. "See, it's right: one-two-three-four-off. It doesn't change."

Troy watched the flashes carefully.

One-two-three-four-off. One-two-three-four-off. One-two-three-four-off. "Okay, so maybe I did count wrong."

Then he muttered, "but I know I didn't."

*****

Across the river, in the second guest room, on the third floor of their aunt's house in Southport, Sam and Becky carefully watched the beam of the Oak Island Lighthouse.

"Right there!" said Sam. "Did you see it?"

Chapter 2
Too Long

"What's a sea turtle sanctuary? Isn't a sanctuary a church? And why does it say Caswell Beach? I thought we were going to Oak Island."

Sam was watching the signs on the road *very* closely.

"Are we almost there? I think the last sign said four miles, and I know we've already been four miles."

"Calm down, Sam," said Becky who was almost two years older than her brother.

"Caswell Beach is the name of a town on Oak Island. There's also another town on Oak Island called...well, it's called Oak Island, which makes it a little confusing."

"A little?" said Sam.

Becky ignored Sam. 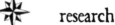 "A sanctuary *is* a church or a holy place, but it also means a safe place for sea turtles—they're an endangered species, you know."

✦ **research**
(REE-surch)
Information collected about a topic. Some people use only the internet sites to do research, but you can also read books and magazine articles, watch videos, and talk to people.

"*I* know that, Becky. You're not the only one who goes to school. I just wish we could go faster. We came all the way from California to see Troy and Andrew, and now we're going to be late."

Mom, Dad, Sam, and Becky were on vacation in North Carolina, where Mom and

Dad were also doing **research** for their book about lighthouses.

"Just chill, Sam!" Becky said. "We've got two whole weeks on Oak Island. The speed limit here is 35 miles an hour, and if Dad goes any faster, he might get another speeding ticket."

"In my defense," said Dad. "I was only going 35 when that nice motorcycle police officer pulled me over."

"That's great, Mike," said Mom, "but the speed limit there was 25."

"I did realize that—just as soon as the officer pointed it out," said Dad nodding his head.

"Will the Jamisons be at the lighthouse?" asked Becky.

19

"Yes," said Mom. "Mr. Jamison even set up a special tour so we can go to the top of the lighthouse today. Look! The lighthouse is getting bigger and bigger. We should be there any minute."

Chapter 3
Too Plain

"It's not a very pretty lighthouse," Sam said, with a little **disdain** in his voice.

"I mean, it looks like somebody said, 'Hey, let's build a lighthouse as fast as we can,' and then they

> **disdain**
> (diss-DANE)
> A feeling of dislike or no respect.

did. I'm surprised they even bothered to paint it three colors."

"They aren't even colors really," said Becky. "Just gray, white, and black, and you're right, it's ugly. I'm sorry, but there's just no other way to describe it."

"Certainly there's another way to describe it." Dad shaded his eyes as he looked toward the towering column. "It's stately…it's proud…it's elegant in its simplicity…its clean lines are poetic. Don't you think so, Alice?" he asked, turning to look at Mom.

"I don't know that I'd go that far," said Mom. "I appreciate all the work it does, but

I have to agree with Sam. It's certainly not going to win any beauty contests."

She squinted up at the slim column ahead of them. "Just think about the lighthouse we saw at Cape Hatteras. It has a very nice shape and a pretty candy-cane, barber-pole striped pattern. And then there's the lighthouse at Cape Lookout with that lovely diamond pattern."

"I guess beauty is in the eye of the beholder and not the builder," said Dad as he stopped to let a family with folding chairs, coolers, and lots of sand toys cross the road in front of them.

"I expect if you were a sailor who had lost his way and you saw those three sturdy layers, you'd think it was the most beautiful lighthouse in the world—even if it was a little plain."

When the beach-going family was safe on the other side, Dad continued down the road. "You know," he said, "this isn't the first lighthouse that was built around here."

narrator
(NE'ER-ate-tur)
Someone who is telling a story. A narrator often gives the reader (or the audience) background information.

Becky rolled her eyes and Sam groaned out loud. Whenever Dad started a sentence with "You know…" and started talking in his (as Sam called it) **narrator** voice, he could go on *forever*!

"Yep," said Dad taking a deep breath, "this lighthouse is just a youngster. The first  real lighthouse for Oak Island wasn't even *on* Oak Island. It was over on Smith Island—or, as they call it today, Bald Head Island."

"There's actually an island called Bald Head Island?" Sam knew that Dad liked to stretch the truth a bit—especially if it made for a better story. "I suppose they named it for the bald head that someone found in the middle of the island?"

"Something like that—only the bald head was a sand dune—in fact, several of them. The dunes were the tallest spot on the island. The story is that ships going to Wilmington looked for the island with the bald heads because it marked the entrance to the Cape Fear River."

"But, if they already had a lighthouse on Bald Head Island, why did they need one here?" Sam was determined to get Dad to the end of his story as soon as possible. Sometimes asking questions helped move things along.

"Well, the first lighthouse they built on Bald Head Island got washed away before it was even 20 years old. So in 1817, they tore down what was left of it and built a new one. It's called Old Baldy and it's still standing over there on Bald Head Island."

"I repeat," Sam said. "Why did they need a lighthouse on Oak Island if they already had one on Bald Head Island?"

"Well, the problem was that those first lighthouses just marked the entrance to the Cape Fear River and they weren't very tall.

25

They couldn't be seen far enough out to sea to warn ships about the **treacherous** Frying Pan Shoals."

★ **treacherous**
(TRETCH-er-us)
Extremely dangerous, often with the danger hidden from view.

"Okay, Dad, now you're just making things up to see if we're listening," said Becky. "I'm not sure what a shoal is, but I really don't think there's such a thing as Frying Pan Shoals."

"I don't know, Becky," said Sam, "these are the same people that thought Bald Head was a good name for an island. Why not Frying Pan Shoals?"

"Your father is absolutely correct," said Mom. "A shoal is a part of the ocean that has shallow water and sandbars that move around a lot. Shoals can be extremely dangerous for ships. The shoals off Cape Fear are called Frying Pan Shoals because the area with the sandbars is shaped like a frying pan."

"The people that name these things have a *lot* of imagination," Becky whispered to Sam. Then she said, "Go on, Dad."

"Well, to help the sailors get safely through Frying Pan Shoals, the U.S. Government decided to anchor a lightship out there in 1854. That was a pretty good idea, and for almost a hundred years— except during the Civil War—a Frying Pan Shoals Lightship was on duty.

"By the way, they eventually replaced the lightship with a light tower, and one of the old lightships is now a restaurant at a dock in New York City! The funny thing is that when the government eventually retired the light tower, somebody bought that too! Now it's a place for people who like those adventure vacations."

"Cool!" said Becky. "Where is it? Can we go see it?"

"It's way out in the Atlantic Ocean about 30 miles east of Southport," Mom said. "To see it, you'd have to go by helicopter or boat. There's no land, just the tower— swaying with the storms and the waves and moving up and down, up and down, up..."

Mom looked a little green as she swallowed and said, "I don't think we'll be visiting."

"So, Dad," Sam asked, "when did they finally build the Oak Island Lighthouse?"

"I was just getting to that, son. You see, the Cape Fear area was attracting more and more ships from all over the world. The lightship was helpful, but it couldn't be seen from very far away. The people in charge of the lighthouses and lightships were worried that, in a big storm or hurricane, the lightship might blow free of its **moorings**— right when it was needed the most.

moorings
(MOUR-rings)
Lines or chains attached to anchors that hold a ship in place.

"So, they decided to build a taller lighthouse. It took seven years, but in 1901, they finally got permission to build a 150-foot lighthouse called the Cape Fear Lighthouse…"

"Finally!" said Sam.

"…also over on Bald Head Island," finished Dad.

"It's not fair!" Sam said. "Why does Bald Head get all the lighthouses?"

Sam looked at the Oak Island Lighthouse growing taller right in front of him and added, "Well, I guess they didn't get *all*

of the lighthouses. What happened to the Cape Fear Lighthouse, Dad? Is it still there?"

"Nope, they blew it up! Well, they did, Alice," he said as Mom raised her eyebrows.

"They blew it up right after they fired up this baby. At the time, the Oak Island Lighthouse was the brightest lighthouse in the United States and the second brightest in the world. Even today, ships can see it from 24 miles out at sea and *I* think it's beautiful."

But Sam and Becky had stopped listening, because, while Dad was talking, he'd parked the car in the small parking area right beside all 148 feet of the Oak Island Lighthouse.

Chapter 4
Too Weird

"It makes me dizzy," said Sam, looking straight up at the lighthouse.

"Look," said Becky, "you can see the light beam even from way down here."

"Yep," said Dad. "When sailors see that one-two-three-four-off flash pattern, they know right where they are."

"Hey, Dad," said Sam with a quick glance at Becky, "have you ever heard of a lighthouse that changed its flash in the middle of the night?"

31

Becky made a face at Sam and shook her head at him. But it was too late.

"Well," said Dad, "most of the lighthouses today are computerized. To change the flash pattern, you'd have to change the computer."

"See, Sam. I told you it wasn't possible."

"Now if we were living a couple hundred years ago," said Dad, "it would be another  story. Lighthouse keepers had to go up to the top of the lighthouse and light the oil lamps at night and during storms. So, you might see a mistake or two when the lamp blew out or if the lighthouse keeper had a problem lighting it."

"See, Becky. I told you it was possible."

"And," Dad continued, "if you were a pirate trying to signal to other pirates or trying to trick a ship into running aground in the shallow waters, then sure, the light flashes could change."

"Pirates?" said Sam. "Were there pirates around here?"

"Only some of the most **notorious** pirates in the business," said Dad, "including Edward Teach—better known as Blackbeard."

Dad turned back to get his hat from the car. "Yep, those pirates were tricky. Sometimes they lit extra signal lights or covered up the real lights. The sailors would get confused about where the deep water was, and their ship would get stuck on a sandbar. Then the pirates would row out to the ship and take the cargo— everything from spices to guns to gold. Sometimes they even kidnapped the crew and made them work on the pirate ship!"

notorious
(no-TOR-ee-us)
Something or someone famous, but for bad reasons.

"Gee," said Sam with a shiver. "I'm glad ol' Blackbeard isn't around anymore."

"I wouldn't be too sure about that," said Dad, half to himself. "Stranger things have happened."

"Mom, is it okay if we go over and check out the **Coast Guard** station?" asked Becky.

Coast Guard

(COHST gard)
The U.S. Coast Guard is part of the U.S. military responsible for guarding and protecting the waterways of the United States— anywhere that land meets water, including oceans, lakes, and rivers.

"That's fine, dear. Just stay where you can see us. Mr. and Mrs. Jamison and the kids will be here soon."

Sam followed Becky away from the lighthouse. "Why did you make a face at me? Aren't we going to tell them what we saw last night?"

Becky gave Sam another warning look as she walked down the road to the driveway in front of the fenced Coast Guard station. Two huge **buoys**—one red and one green—guarded the entrance.

buoys (BOO-eez) Floating markers (usually anchored in the water) that warn of danger or mark a safe path for boats.

Becky wrinkled her forehead and turned back to look up at the lighthouse. "I don't know, Sam. Maybe we *didn't* see anything. We were all the way over in Southport. Maybe we just missed the last flash."

"No! It happened, and it happened more than once! After the first time, I started counting very carefully: One-two-three-four-off. One-two-three-four-off. And then it was one-two-three-off. A few minutes later it did it again. I'm sure the last flash was missing!"

Sam had started out whispering to Becky, but now he was talking loud enough for others to hear. "I didn't count wrong, Becky. We both saw it. You know we did!"

"Boy, am I glad to hear that," said a voice behind them, "because I saw it too!"

Becky and Sam spun around to see a boy about their age wearing a sky-blue baseball cap and a T-shirt with a big green and gray sea turtle on the front.

"*What* did you see?" asked Becky carefully.

"I saw the same thing you saw," said the boy. He put his head to one side and smiled. "Didn't I?"

"What do you think we saw?" asked Sam.

"You know—the thing that doesn't just happen. Last night. My brother said I made a mistake counting the flashes, but I didn't. You saw it too, didn't you?"

"What do you think it means?" Sam was so excited that someone else had seen the odd flashes that he couldn't pretend any longer.

Becky held up both hands. "Hold on, Sam. Before we get too excited, maybe we should ask the lighthouse people if they know about any problems with their computer or with the lighthouse last night."

"I'm climbing to the top of the lighthouse today," said the boy, "so I can ask them then. The lighthouse guides are great and they love it when you ask questions. By the way, my name is Troy. What's yours?"

"My name is Sam and this is my sister, Becky. We're here with my mom and dad and we're going to climb the lighthouse too—as soon as my dad's friend and his family get here."

"My brother Andrew is over there with my mom and dad and my baby sister, Eden." Troy pointed to the lighthouse parking lot and a boy that looked just like him.

Becky looked where Troy pointed and saw Dad laughing and talking to a tall man holding a little girl. A woman with a friendly smile laughed out loud with Mom.

"I think *you* are our dad's friend's son," she said. "Is your dad's name Ed Jamison?"

"Yep," said Troy. "Are you from California?"

"Yep," said Becky.

"When did you get here?"

"We flew into Raleigh yesterday," said

Sam, "and drove down here to stay with our aunt in Southport. This morning we drove over the Oak Island Bridge to get to the lighthouse."

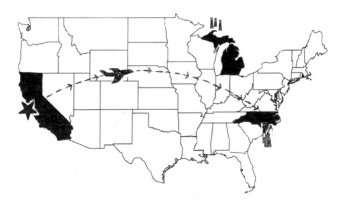

"Our mom and dad write books about lighthouses so we end up spending a lot of our vacations visiting lighthouses," sighed Becky.

"Yeah, and the last time we visited a lighthouse, it had a ghost," said Sam in a loud whisper. "Maybe this one does too."

"Shhh," warned Becky as Dad and Mom came over to meet Troy and introduce Sam and Becky to Troy's family.

"Hi, Troy," said Dad. "I see you've met Sam and Becky. "Were they telling you about the ghost they met at the Copper Harbor Lighthouse when we were in Michigan?"

"Dad!"

"A ghost?" said Troy's dad. "Maybe there's one in the Oak Island Lighthouse too. We'll have to ask Lighthouse Bob about it, but right now we'd better get back. I think they're about to start the tour."

Chapter 5
Inside the Lighthouse

"They're more like ladders, even though we call them steps," said Lighthouse Bob, one of the tour guides for the Oak Island Lighthouse. He stood on the front porch of the lighthouse, greeting visitors and explaining the best way to climb the steep steps inside.

"You don't notice it so much when you're going up, but when you come down, you can't go down facing forward like you would on regular steps. You have to climb down backwards, like you're on a ladder."

"Remember," said Liz, the lighthouse guide who led the way up the first ladder, "it was the Coast Guard who took care of the lighthouse when it was first built. Those folks like ladders better than steps because they can use them to get down preeeety fast. Kinda' like a firefighter going down a pole."

Lighthouse Bob climbed up the ladder after Liz. He stopped, but she went on up to the next level. Once everyone had climbed up to the first landing, Lighthouse Bob started to talk.

"The U.S. Government started building the Oak Island Lighthouse in 1957," said Lighthouse Bob. "Shippers in the area wanted a stronger light to mark the Cape Fear River, but they also needed a light to help them avoid Frying Pan Shoals."

Troy put his hand up. "Why did ships need help? Why didn't they just look at a map, turn in at the right place, and drive up the river until they got to Wilmington?"

"Well, it's not that simple," answered Lighthouse Bob.

"Most parts of the Cape Fear River are too shallow for the big **container ships** that travel up to Wilmington. So, the U. S. Army Corps of Engineers—that's the part of the Army that takes care of bridges, dams, rivers and things like that—digs a big ditch, called a *channel,* right in the middle of the river so the ships can go up to Wilmington and then back out to sea."

container ship
(kon-TAIN-er ship) A ship that carries cargo in "truck-sized" containers that can be quickly unloaded onto trailer trucks and railcars without being opened. Malcom McLean from Maxton, North Carolina, came up with this idea while he was waiting for his cargo to be unloaded onto his truck box by box.

Lighthouse Bob shook his head. "Digging out the channel is a never-ending job

because the ocean keeps filling it in with new sand. The bigger ships hire tugboats to guide them down the river and out past Frying Pan Shoals. If they didn't, they'd get stuck just like the old sailing ships did."

Lighthouse Bob rubbed his chin. "In fact, there's a story that one of the old sailing ships that ran aground right near here belonged to Stede Bonnet, the gentleman pirate."

"Why did they call him the gentleman pirate?" asked Andrew. He was interested in everything about pirates.

"Well… because he was, well…" Lighthouse Bob sighed. "The fact is that while Stede Bonnet was a pretty good gentleman, he wasn't a very good pirate."

"I've never heard of a good pirate," said Troy. "Aren't all pirates mean?"

"No, I don't mean *kind*. I mean he wasn't very good at being a pirate. You see, Stede

44

Bonnet owned a big sugarcane plantation down on the island of Barbados—way south of Florida. He had a wife and kids and friends, but he just wasn't very happy. So, one day he decided to be a pirate."

"How do you just *decide* to be a pirate?" asked Andrew.

"Well, most of the time pirates don't have much money, so they steal a ship and kidnap the crew to work for them. But Stede Bonnet didn't know much about pirating, and he was already rich, so he bought a ship and hired a crew to work on his pirate ship. He even loaded his whole library of books on board the ship. Then, in his elegant clothes— complete with the powdered wig that most gentlemen wore at the time—off he sailed.

45

Lighthouse Bob took a deep breath. "After a couple of years of pirating—including some time spent with ol' Blackbeard himself—Stede Bonnet was captured right here on the banks of the Cape Fear River. They took him down to Charleston, South Carolina for his trial. He almost got away once—by dressing up as a lady— but they caught him, and eventually, they hanged him."

nag
(NAG)
Someone who is always reminding others about things they need to do, often in a bullying kind of way.

Lighthouse Bob sighed. "I know he deserved to be hanged—after all, he stole from the merchants and sometimes he burned their ships—but I think he wasn't that bad of a guy, just unhappy. Everybody said his wife was a bit of a **nag**."

Lighthouse Bob rubbed his chin. "I think he didn't want to be a pirate as much as he just wanted to go off on an adventure and get away from her."

After a moment or two, Lighthouse Bob continued his story. He spoke in a low, soft voice, and everyone leaned forward to hear.

"Some say that Stede Bonnet's ghost still haunts this area, guarding his treasure. People also say that the ghost of Blackbeard—the world's meanest pirate in my opinion—also haunts the waters around Cape Fear. They say Blackbeard is looking for Bonnet's treasure from all those years ago."

When Lighthouse Bob finished the story of Stede Bonnet, no one said a word.

It was a full minute before the lighthouse guide clapped his hands together and said, "All right, then. Enough about pirates and ghosts. Let's climb this lighthouse!"

He pointed at Mr. Jamison and then pointed up.

Mr. Jamison put his foot on the first step and started up the ladder with Troy, Sam, Andrew, Becky, Mom, and Dad lining up behind him.

Chapter 6
Going Up

"If you have any questions along the way, feel free to ask them," called out Lighthouse Bob. "I always say there's no such thing as a bad question!"

"How far is it to the top?" asked Sam, looking straight up the slim column of concrete.

"Well," said Lighthouse Bob, "the lighthouse is 148 feet tall, but the light is actually 169 feet above sea level because the lighthouse was built on a little hill. Most

✳ **reinforced concrete**

(re-in-FORST KON-kreet) Concrete (a building material usually made out of cement, sand, and water) that contains steel bars or metal netting to increase its strength.

people only get to go to this first level, but today you're going all the way to the top—that's 131 steps."

While Mom waited for her turn to go up the steps, she turned to Lighthouse Bob and asked, "Do they always paint the inside when they paint the outside?" She pointed to the place where the first fat gray stripe ended and the second fat stripe—this one white—began.

"Ma'am," said Lighthouse Bob proudly, "this lighthouse has never been painted and

never will be. It is built entirely of **reinforced concrete**. The builders poured it one section at a time and kept pouring, 24 hours a day for 7 days until it was all done. They used plain gray cement for the first layer, they added white cement to make the second layer, and for the third layer, they added black coloring right into the cement as they mixed it. Because the color is in the concrete, the stripes never fade and the lighthouse never needs painting. Pretty smart, don't you think?"

When it was his turn, Dad raced up the first few steps on the ladder, but he soon slowed down. Climbing straight up was hard work.

By the time he got to the middle of the second ladder he was moving even slower. He stopped to look out the window and catch his breath, and then slowly **trudged** up the next ladder.

trudged
(TRUHJED)
Walked slowly with a lot of effort.

"Mike, are you okay down there?" Mom was almost to the top, but Dad was just finishing up his third set of steps.

"Just taking some pictures, dear," Dad called up to her.

"But, Dad," Sam called down from up above, "there's no window there."

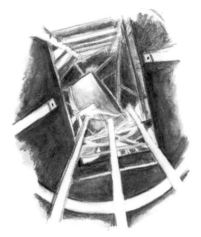

"I don't recall asking for your opinion, young man. I know there's no window. I'm taking pictures of the *inside* of the lighthouse." Dad sounded **offended**.

Troy laughed and then said to Sam, "And I thought *my* dad took weird pictures."

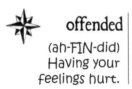

offended
(ah-FIN-did)
Having your feelings hurt.

Sam just shook his head and kept climbing.

"You just wait," called Dad. "These will be the coolest pictures from our whole trip and everyone will want to see them. And I *may* decide not to share them, since everyone is being such a **critic**."

Dad was right. When you looked straight up, things looked crazy. People near the top of the tower looked tiny, and everyone's feet looked twice as big as their heads.

critic

(KRI tik)

Someone whose job is to judge and give an opinion of something, such as movies, food, music, or art.

Dad snapped many, many, *many* pictures before he was fully rested. Then, he took a drink from his water bottle and started climbing the ladder again.

Chapter 7
Wow!

Troy followed Lighthouse Liz and Mr. Jamison as they stepped outside at the top of the lighthouse.

"Wow!"

"Wow is right!" said Sam right behind him.

"Wow!" said Andrew as he stepped out from the shadowed steps onto the narrow walkway that curved all the way around the lighthouse.

When Becky stepped outside, she immediately looked straight down to the lighthouse entrance and waved to Mrs. Jamison and Eden.

"Wow," she said to the others, "this is great!"

"You can see everything!" said Mom behind them. Mom was a great admirer of high places and great views. "Wow!"

Everyone was enjoying the amazing feeling of being up so high when Dad finally put his head through the door.

"Here...I...am," he said, breathing hard. "No worry...fine. Don't...wait, I'm...Wow!"

exhilirating
(x-HILL-er-
ate-ing)
Happy,
wonderful, and
exciting—all at
the same time!

It is an **exhilarating** feeling to compete with the seagulls for a place in the sky. Everyone breathed deeply and looked at the incredible views in front of them. And then they started trading places.

"Look over here! I think I can see all the way up the river to Wilmington."

"See how that big container ship is staying right in the middle of the river between the buoys? Just like she's supposed to be."

"Look at the ocean! From here you can see where the deeper water starts—look how much darker it is. I sure hope that captain sees it too."

"Look at those clouds!" said Troy. "I think we're going to have a thunderstorm this afternoon."

Out toward the ocean, towering, light gray **cumulonimbus** clouds were gathering on the horizon.

"I believe you're right, Troy," said Dad. "Looks like we're in for some rain. It's just like that old saying,

> *When the wind is from the south,*
> *it brings rain in its mouth.*

"Wait a minute, Dad" said Becky. "The coast of North Carolina faces east, so aren't those clouds on the eastern horizon?"

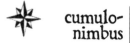

cumulo-nimbus

(CUME-u-lo-nim-bus)
Also known as thunderstorm clouds, these are cumulous clouds that have collected energy from the condensation of the cloud's water vapor.

"You're right, Becky," said Mr. Jamison, "most of North Carolina's coast faces east. But one of the nice things about this little stretch of the coast is that it faces south. It's one of the few places where you can watch the sun rise *and* set over the ocean."

"Wait a minute," started Andrew, "when we were up at the **Outer Banks,** we saw… No, I guess we just saw the sun *rise* over the water."

Outer Banks
(out-er BANKS)
The 200-mile long string of very skinny islands that are the eastern border of North Carolina and separate the Atlantic Ocean from the Currituck Sound, the Albemarle Sound, and the Pamlico Sound.

"Okay, but in California we can see…" Sam stopped. "I guess you're right, Mr. Jamison. We just see the sun *setting* over the Pacific Ocean. It's pretty cool that we get to see both from Oak Island."

"Just part of the magic here," said Dad. He was once again clicking and taking pictures of every possible view, at every possible angle.

"Look, Becky." Sam said, as he pointed across the river. "There's Southport. It's not *that* far away. See? There's Aunt Lexi's house right there."

He raised his eyebrows meaningfully.

"You're right," said Becky. "It's pretty close. I can even see that ice cream place Dad wanted to try."

"You're going to have to be a lot more specific than that, Becky," laughed Mom. "Dad wants to try ice cream places all over the country. You might as well be talking about Copper Harbor."

"Okay, the ice cream place he wanted to try in Southport."

"That narrows it down to two," said Mr. Jamison. "Keep going."

"The place in the park that faces the river," said Becky carefully. "The one that has the sign about homemade banana ice cream."

"Now you're talking," said Dad. "I remember that place. I also remember that Ed promised Eden a trip over to Southport when we finished our lighthouse climb. I'm going down! Who else wants ice cream?"

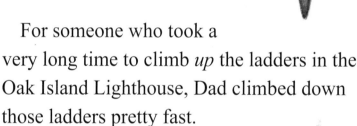

For someone who took a very long time to climb *up* the ladders in the Oak Island Lighthouse, Dad climbed down those ladders pretty fast.

Chapter 8
S O S

As Troy waited for the others to climb down, he leaned on the railing that surrounded the ledge of the lighthouse and looked down. The Atlantic Ocean stretched out in front of him, and to his right were houses—each with a long **boardwalk** to the beach.

boardwalk
(BORED-walk)
A raised walkway, usually wooden, that lets people walk over wet, sandy, or dangerous areas.

At low tide there was a lot of beach between the waves and the sand dunes that protected the houses, but right now, at high tide, the beach was almost gone, and the water went right up to the sand dunes. It looked like the houses were getting ready to go wading in the waves.

Looking down to his left, Troy saw the old house that was the original Coast Guard station. It was someone's home now. There were no houses right below the lighthouse, just a long boardwalk that pushed its way through a jungle of wax myrtle bushes covered with tangled vines, and then out to a platform surrounded by **sea oats**.

If you wanted to, you could go down the steps to the beach. Or, you could just sit on the bench and watch the beach, the water, and the waves in front of you.

"Those vines are everywhere," mumbled Troy. From up here everything looked soft and green, but he knew the vines had tough, stringy branches—some even had thorns!

The twisted, bare wood of the branches and vines seemed to form letters with their kinks, curves, and (sometimes) straight lines. In fact…Troy squinted and stared at the vines below. Then he rubbed his eyes and looked again.

"Sam!" he yelled. "Sam, look at this!"

sea oats

(see ohts)
A type of grass that grows on the East Coast and the Gulf Coast in the United States.

Like wax myrtle bushes, sea oats love hot sun, salty water, and sand. Their long roots hold the sand in place and help protect the sand dunes—especially during storms and hurricanes.
It is against the law to pick sea oats in North Carolina!

Sam's foot was on the first step to go down the ladder, but when he heard Troy call, he came back outside. Troy was standing there, pointing down at the bushes.

Sam looked where Troy was pointing. Then he took off his glasses, rubbed his eyes, put his glasses back on, and looked again. He glanced at Troy, and they both called out, "Becky! Becky, come here!"

Becky popped her head back out the door. "What? They want us to go down now. Come on!"

"Becky, come here and look!" said Sam.

Becky sighed and rolled her eyes, but she walked back onto the ledge. "I've already seen all the views, Sam. They're great, but we need to go. Dad's going to…"

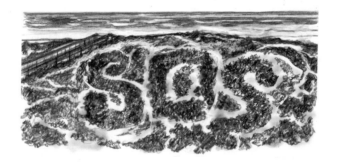

Becky eyes got huge when she looked down where Troy and Sam were pointing.

Right there, in the middle of the bushes, as clear as day, the branches and vines spelled out *SOS*.

SOS

(es oh es)
An international symbol for help based on the **Morse Code** for the letters S (• • •), O (− − −), and S again (• • •). The series of dots and dashes standing for the letters SOS (• • • − − − • • •) were easy to send over the telegraph and easy to remember.

"We're glad you like the lighthouse, kids, but it's time to go. We have to close it up for the day." Lighthouse Liz was checking for other visitors as she spoke to Troy, Sam, and Becky.

"But, ma'am," said Troy, "look over here. There's a message in the myrtle bushes."

"Oh, my yes," laughed Liz, not even looking down. "We're always talking to people who see letters in the wax myrtle bushes. I saw an *L* the other day—you know, *L* for Liz—at least I like to think it was an *L*."

Morse Code

(mors kode)
A code developed by Samuel Morse in 1853 that changes the letters of the alphabet into a series of dots and dashes that can easily be transmitted over the telegraph.

Sam, Becky, and Troy looked again at the bushes and then at each other. The message was gone!

"Oh, my!" said Liz. "There's Lighthouse Bob calling again. We've got to get y'all down. You come back and see us sometime, okay?"

Chapter 9
Shopping in Southport

Homemade banana ice cream is really good. Milkshakes made from homemade banana ice cream are just as good and are sometimes a better choice on a hot day.

While Dad, Mr. Jamison, and Eden—still slurping the last bits of their milkshakes—walked over to the Southport pier, Mom, Mrs. Jamison, and the older kids wandered in and out of the stores that shared the block with the ice-cream shop.

"Let's go in here," called Becky as she climbed the steps to a little shop called *Pirate Loot*. A string of bells on the door jangled as she opened the door into a cool dark room.

"It's kinda like a pirate's cave," said Andrew. "Look at that treasure chest. It's full of chocolate coins and candy jewels!"

Becky saw a stack of books on a table by the window and drifted over to look at them more closely.

"Look," said Troy. "This parrot sits on your shoulder and squawks when you talk to him. Try it, Sam."

Mom joined Becky at the table of books. "Are these journals?" she asked as Becky picked up a book with a picture of sea oats, sand, and waves on the cover.

Becky opened the book to see empty pages—just waiting for someone to write on them.

"Is this the size you wanted?" Mom asked. "I know you and Sam were trying to find

journals for this trip."

"Sam found a journal he liked before we left," replied Becky, "But I'm still trying to find the right one."

"Are those journals?" asked Sam. He and Troy peeked over Becky's shoulder. "I started writing in mine on the plane. Do you guys have journals?"

"I do," Andrew answered, "but I don't think Troy has one."

"I had one in school," said Troy, "and we had to write in it every day. But it's summer now, so I'm not writing in it any more. How about you Becky?"

"Well, the one I was writing in is full, so Mom said she would buy me a new one. I think I'm going to get this one with the beach and the waves on it."

"You know," Troy said slowly, "I never thought I'd want to write in a journal while I was on vacation, but this vacation is different. Maybe I *would* like to have a journal—you know, just to write down things that happen." He grinned at Sam.

Mrs. Jamison came up behind Troy just in time to hear his last words. "Sweetheart, if you tell me you'll write in a journal, I'll be happy to buy one for you."

"That's a deal," said Troy. "Can I get any one I want?"

"If you promise to write in it, you can get two!" said his mom.

"Funny, Mom," said Troy, looking like he didn't think it was funny at all. He poked through the books on the table, and then picked up one that had a picture of the Oak Island Lighthouse on the cover. When he opened the journal, the paper inside was a light brown that had been printed to look like it was very old.

"I think I'll get this one." said Troy. "The inside kinda' looks like the paper they used when they made treasure maps. Maybe I'll learn how to write like they did on those old maps so my journal will look like it was written by a pirate!"

decipher
(dee-SY-fur)
Decoding something that's written in a code or in very messy handwriting.

"As long as you can read it," Mrs. Jamison said. She winked at the others. "We may have the next great American author right here! It would be a shame if we couldn't read his book because we couldn't **decipher** his handwriting."

"Aw, come on, Mom," said Troy. "You know Andrew's handwriting is worse than mine."

"And Dad's is worse than both of ours put together," said Andrew, not to be outdone.

Mrs. Jamison sighed. "They're right," she said to Mom. "Ed's handwriting *is* **atrocious**. If he wasn't a doctor, he'd never get away with it. Thank goodness he does most of his work on the computer now."

atrocious
(uh-TRO-shush)
Really, really, really, really bad.

While Mom and Mrs. Jamison paid for the journals, Sam, Troy, Becky, and Andrew waited for them and looked at the postcards in the rack by the door.

"Hey, you guys," Sam asked. "What's a dogwood?"

"It's a tree," Troy said. "It's the state tree of North Carolina. "

"Are there different kinds? You know, like poodle dogwoods or golden retriever dogwoods?" Sam tried to keep a straight face, but he couldn't hold back and grinned.

"Yeah, that's right," laughed Andrew. "And the only way you can tell them apart is by their bark!"

When Mrs. Jamison handed Troy's journal to the man at the counter, an orange piece of paper fell out and fluttered to the floor.

"What's this?" asked Troy, picking up the paper and handing it to the clerk.

"Oh you can keep it," said the clerk waving it back to Troy. "It's just a **flyer** about the Pirate Days they're having next week over on Bald Head Island. Are you folks going to be around for another week?"

flyer
(FLY-ur)
An advertisement on a piece of paper that tells about an upcoming event.

"Yes," said Mom. "Actually for a little longer than that—two weeks and three weekends!"

"Well, go over to Pirate Days if you can. It's always a big hit with the kids."

As they followed Mom and Mrs. Jamison out of the door, Sam, Becky, Andrew, and Troy looked at the flyer.

"We can show it to Dad," said Sam. "I'm pretty sure he and Mom are planning to go to Bald Head Island to see the lighthouse over there. Maybe they'll go next week, and then we can all go too."

Troy folded the flyer and started to put it in his pocket.

"What's that on the back?" asked Andrew.

"On the back of what?"

"On the back of the pirate flyer. There's something written on it."

Troy unfolded the paper and turned it over. On the back was a grid of letters in a square. "It's some kind of puzzle," he said.

X	F	L	T	Y	I	Q	L
L	H	V	A	F	G	C	B
O	A	E	N	T	U	S	L
K	T	I	B	J	B	Q	M
R	A	Y	A	W	O	R	D
U	Y	F	N	B	F	Z	4
S	R	F	J	L	U	M	I
L	A	G	L	F	L	M	G
A	O	H	F	O	T	Q	N

"It looks like somebody drew it by hand." He handed the paper to Sam.

"It looks like one of those scrambled word puzzles," said Sam.

"Let me see," said Becky. "I love word puzzles, especially the word searches—you know the ones with rows of letters in one big square." She looked at the paper. "I don't think this is a word search—they usually have more letters. Maybe it's a code."

"A code? Andrew is great with codes!" said Troy. "Give it to him and see if he can figure it out."

77

"Are you kids ready to go?" called Mrs. Jamison. "Eden needs a nap and so do your fathers."

Becky stuffed the flyer in her pocket and everyone piled into the van to go back across the bridge to their beach house on Oak Island.

Chapter 10
Puzzled

"I have an idea," said Sam as he, Troy, and Becky walked along the beach early the next morning. "Let's write the puzzle on the sand so we can all look at it together."

The sun was just coming up behind the lighthouse and the sand was washed clean, with only a few tracks from sandpipers and seagulls and from dogs taking their owners for a morning run.

"That's a great idea," said Becky, pulling the flyer with the puzzle out of her pocket.

"I'll call out the letters. Who wants to write?"

So Becky read from the paper, and Sam and Troy wrote the letters in rows on the hard sand.

"Here comes Andrew," said Troy, sitting back on his heels and watching his brother run down the beach toward them.

"What are you guys doing?" Andrew bent over with his hands on his knees trying to catch his breath. It was a long way to the beach house and he had run as fast as he could the whole way.

"We're still trying to figure out the puzzle. We thought we'd write the letters on the beach so we could study it together. What are you doing?"

"I have an idea about the puzzle," said Andrew still breathing heavily. "I think it *is* a code. Have you ever seen those codes that have a bunch of letters, and then you have a key—like a number—to tell you which letters to use?"

"Oh, I get it," Sam said. "Like if the key is five, you count the letters and every fifth letter is part of the message."

"Exactly," said Andrew.

"Okay," said Troy, "but how do you know what the key is?"

"That's the part I think I just figured out," said Andrew. "What's the thing that started all of this?"

"You mean the lighthouse?" asked Becky.

"Yeah," said Andrew. "I didn't see it because I was reading my Blackbeard book, but everyone else saw the lighthouse beam go from four flashes to three, right? The message in the bushes had three letters— SOS. And now...well, this is the third clue we've gotten. I think the number three is the key to the puzzle."

"Don't forget there are three stripes on the lighthouse!" Sam was feeling a little left out.

"Well, I don't know if that has anything to do with it, but maybe it does."

"Well, don't just stand there," Sam said. "Let's try it!"

So this time, Andrew and Sam counted, Troy called out the letter they stopped on, and Becky wrote the letter in the sand.

"One, two, three," said Andrew and Sam together.

"L" called out Troy, and Becky wrote an *L* in the sand.

"One, two, three," counted Andrew and Sam.

"I" called Troy. Becky wrote an *I*.

On they went, with Andrew and Sam counting carefully, Troy calling out letters, and Becky writing in the sand until they got to the end of the puzzle.

X	F	L	T	Y	I	Q	L
L	H	V	A	F	G	C	B
O	A	E	N	T	U	S	L
K	T	I	B	J	B	Q	M
R	A	Y	A	W	O	R	D
U	Y	F	N	B	F	Z	4
S	R	F	J	L	U	M	I
L	A	G	L	F	L	M	G
A	O	H	F	O	T	Q	N

"What does it say, Becky?" Everyone gathered around Becky to see what she had written in the sand.

LILACATLIBRARYB4FULLMOON

"That doesn't spell anything," said Sam.

"Wait a minute," said Becky. She knelt down to make a few adjustments to the letters in the sand. "How about now?"

LILAC AT LIBRARY B4 FULL MOON

"Wow!" said Troy. "It *is* a message! What do you think it means?"

"Do you think this message is from the same person who wrote the SOS in the bushes?" asked Becky.

"I don't think a *person* wrote the SOS in the bushes," said Sam.

"If a person didn't write it, then who did?" Troy asked the question, but he didn't really want to hear Sam's answer.

"I think it's a ghost," Sam said firmly. "I think it's a ghost who needs our help and this is the only way the ghost can figure out how to talk to us."

"Maybe it's Blackbeard's ghost," Andrew said in a scary Halloween voice. "Maybe he wants us to help him find a hidden treasure at the library."

"That doesn't make sense," said Becky. "Why would Blackbeard want us to help him? We don't even know him. And why lilacs?"

"What *is* a lilac anyway?" asked Sam.

"It's a flower," said Troy. "I think it's yellow."

"It *is* a flower," said Becky, "but it's not yellow. Most lilacs are lilac color…"

"…oh yeah, light purple," finished Sam. "I guess that makes sense."

"That's about the *only* thing that makes sense right now," grumbled Troy.

"Okay," said Sam, "how about this? Maybe somebody…or *something*…needs help *because* of Blackbeard. Remember what Lighthouse Bob said? Some people think the ghost of Blackbeard is still looking for the treasure of that other pirate guy…

"Stede Bonnet." said Becky.

"Right. The treasure that Stede Bonnet hid from him. Maybe it's Stede Bonnet who needs help because he doesn't want Blackbeard to find his treasure."

"Well," said Andrew, "if that's true, and if Blackbeard has a ghost that's anything like the real Blackbeard, then you guys better not mess with him. He was one scary dude. Even the other pirates were afraid of him."

"Do we have another choice?" asked Troy nervously. "I've never met a ghost, and I'm not sure I want the first ghost I meet to be a pirate—especially not Blackbeard."

"What do you think, Becky?" asked Sam.

"Honestly?" said Becky. "I think we should take a trip to the library."

Chapter 11
Checking Out the Library

"Good morning, Andrew! I see you've brought some friends with you this time. Don't tell me you've already finished that pirate book!"

Mrs. Ellis, the head librarian at the Brunswick County Library in Oak Island peered over her glasses at Troy, Becky, and Sam standing in front of her.

"Good morning, ma'am. Andrew is still reading the pirate book—that's why he's not here. I'm Troy, Andrew's twin brother."

"My goodness gracious! You're the spitting image of Andrew—well, of course you are if you're his twin. It's lovely to meet you, Troy. My name is Mrs. Ellis. We see Andrew in here quite a bit, but I believe this is the first time I've seen you or your friends here. Is that right?"

"Yes, ma'am. This is the first time I've been in your library. These are my friends Becky and Sam. They're visiting from California and we have a question for you. We'd like to know if you have a lilac here at the library."

"Are you all interested in growing lilacs?"

"No, ma'am," said Troy. "We're not interested in growing lilacs, we just want to know if you have a lilac here at the library."

"You mean books about lilacs?" asked Mrs. Ellis, just a bit confused.

"I think we mean a real lilac," said Becky, "but we're not positive what a lilac looks like, so we thought we'd ask if there were any here at the library."

"Well, I've been the librarian here since this library was built and I don't know of any lilacs here. Now, if you go down a couple of blocks to Keziah Street, Miss Ruby has a bunch of lilacs growing in her yard. Of course, they don't look like much now in all this heat, but this past spring they were absolutely gorgeous and she…"

BAM!

Mrs. Ellis and the children jumped.

"*What* was that?" asked Becky.

"What was what, dear?" Mrs. Ellis asked quickly.

"That noise! It sounded like somebody dropped a pile of books on the floor!"

"Oh, *that*. Well, that was…uh…" Mrs. Ellis paused for a few moments, like she was trying to remember the answer to an important question, but then she sighed and her shoulders drooped.

"I can't be sure, but chances are very good that it was several books hitting the floor after being pushed off the shelf."

"Why would somebody do that?" asked Sam. "Wait a minute, there's nobody else here is there? My mother's looking up stuff over there, but I don't think *she* did that."

"No, of course not!"

"But if we're the only ones here," Becky said, "then who is pushing books off the shelf?"

Mrs. Ellis played with the stapler on her desk for a moment and then she cleared her throat and looked up at the ceiling. "Would you believe it was…uh…the wind?"

"But, Mrs. Ellis," said Troy, "we're inside. There's no wind blowing in here."

"I know," said Mrs. Ellis, "but that's what I'm supposed to tell people."

BAM!

Another loud crash came from the bookshelves at the back of the library.

Mrs. Ellis frowned and shook her head. "If he wasn't so mean, I'd go back there and give him a piece of my mind. I'm tired of picking up those same books over and over."

She sniffed and dabbed a tissue to the corner of her eye. "One can only imagine the damage that's being done to their poor little **spines**."

spines
(SPYNZ)
The backbone of the book where the pages are connected to the cover. If you crack the spine of a book (by opening it too wide or treating it roughly), the spine is damaged and pages of the book will start to come out.

"Mrs. Ellis," said Becky gently, "do you think someone is pushing the books off the shelf on purpose?"

"Not just someone, my dear. I'm convinced—and L.C. agrees—that it's the work of Mr. Edward Teach."

She leaned forward and said in a whisper, "I refuse to call him by that vulgar nickname—even though that's what everyone else calls him."

BAM!

Mrs. Ellis narrowed her eyes and raised one eyebrow. Then she straightened up and called out to the back of the library. "FINE then! *Blackbeard!* Is that what you want?"

Angry now, Mrs. Ellis didn't bother to lower her voice. "Mr. Blackbeard and his crew terrorized ships in the Atlantic for more than two years. When his pirates saw a ship, they would take down their pirate

flag and raise the flag of a friendly ship. But then— when it was too late for the poor, unsuspecting ship to escape— the pirates would raise Mr. Blackbeard's pirate flag and attack. Not only was he mean, but he was sneaky."

Mrs. Ellis sat down stiffly at her desk and took off her glasses, letting them hang down on the beaded chain around her neck. She folded her hands on top of her desk.

"According to the library's board of directors, ghosts do not exist. So, obviously the library doesn't have a ghost—especially one as mean as Mr. Blackbeard."

Mrs. Ellis leaned forward to whisper. "Perhaps they should come and visit sometime when somebody asks for a book about Stede Bonnet. *That's* when Mr. Blackbeard gets really angry."

BAM!

"Oh, for goodness sakes! I don't know why he's having such a fit today. You're only here to ask about lilacs."

"Well, actually," said Troy slowly, "we do have a few questions about pirates."

Sam poked him in the ribs.

"Okay," said Troy. "We have questions about Stede Bonnet."

BAM!

"Well! That does change things a bit. Of course the library has books you could look at—although they're probably all on the floor now." Mrs. Ellis glared at the shelves at the back of the library.

"However, if you want to know about Stede Bonnet, your best source of information is L.C. She knows just about everything there is to know about Stede Bonnet. She's usually here in the mornings, but today they needed someone to help out over at the museum in Southport. I'm sure she'll be working over at the putt-putt tonight, though."

Troy, Sam, and Becky thanked Mrs. Ellis and started outside to wait for Mom. Then Troy turned back.

"Mrs. Ellis, do you happen to know when the next full moon is?"

"Not offhand, dear. It's soon, though. Look at the tide charts right there on the community bulletin board in the lobby as you go outside. That will tell you about the moon."

Becky, Sam, and Troy found the tide chart just where Mrs. Ellis said it would be.

"It says that 99 per cent of the moon will be showing tomorrow night," said Becky. "That's about as full as you can get without being in space."

We have to find those lilacs before tomorrow night then," said Troy.

As they waited outside, Sam turned to

grave
(grayv)
Very serious.
Concerned or very
stern.

Troy with a **grave** face. "Troy? I have a very important question to ask you."

"Is it about Blackbeard? Or Stede Bonnet? I bet it's about the lighthouse isn't it? Is it about why Andrew didn't come with us? I thought he might—he likes libraries—but he really wanted to finish that pirate book and when Andrew starts reading something, it's almost impossible to…"

"Hurry up and ask your question, Sam." Becky laughed as she interrupted Troy. "Otherwise we'll be here all day waiting for Troy to *guess* what you're going to ask."

Sam turned to Troy and looked very serious. "The answer to this question may affect our whole visit to Oak Island."

Troy gulped and looked worried. "Okay, Sam. I'll do my best to give you a good answer. What's the question?"

Sam cleared his throat and took a deep breath. "Before we can go any further, Troy, Becky and I need to know…"

"What?" Troy asked desperately.

"Troy, what is putt-putt?"

Chapter 12
Putt-Putt

As it turns out, what some people call **putt-putt** is miniature golf, like dragon golf or jungle golf or, on Oak Island, around-the-world golf.

Putt-Putt®
(PUTT-putt)
The only patented game of miniature golf, Putt-Putt was started in 1954 by Don Clayton in Fayetteville, North Carolina.

The Around-the-World Golf 'n Games on Oak Island has palm trees, a nine-foot tall stone gorilla, and an elephant that, every once in a while, sprays water on anybody standing close by. There's also a windmill, several mountains, and even a very small Statue of Liberty.

The holes for this miniature golf ranged from very easy (everyone made a hole-in-one except Dad) to the rather difficult windmill hole (where the blades of the windmill kept blocking the hole) to a

✷ **suspiciously**
(su-SPISH-iss-lee)
Something that you don't entirely trust and tend to be careful of.

suspiciously easy hole that turned out to be the target for the elephant when he shot water through his trunk.

The next to the last hole—called a mole hole—had the hole on top of a little hill. It looked like it would be easy to hit the ball into the hole, but it was actually pretty hard to hit the ball so that it stayed up on top of the hill. Everyone had five tries, but no one was able to hit the ball into the mole hole.

Until it was Andrew's turn.

Andrew went last. He had carefully watched everyone else take their five tries. Then, when it was his turn, Andrew tapped his bright orange ball just the right amount.

It went right to the top of the hill…wobbled a bit…and stayed! Then he gently tapped the

ball into the cup.

"How did you do that, son?" Mr. Jamison smiled in surprise, but you could tell he was very proud of Andrew.

"I just watched you guys and then I didn't do what you all did," said Andrew.

"Well, it sure worked," said Dad. "I think you get to be the first one to order ice cream, Andrew. My treat!"

Dad loved ice cream, and Mr. Jamison had been telling Dad about a special royal peach ice cream that could only be found at the Around-the-World Golf 'n Games Ice Cream Shoppe.

"It doesn't surprise me that Mike is buying ice cream for us," said Mom as they all stood in line to order their ice cream, "but it does surprise me that he's letting someone else go first. Andrew, you are a very lucky young man."

"That's right, Andrew," said Dad, "so step right up and order anything you want. This is indeed a special day."

"Andrew always gets the same thing," said Troy. "Don't you, Andrew?"

"Well," said Andrew slowly, "not always. And since this is a special day, I'm going to order something different. No chocolate and **pistachio** in a cone for me this time. Tonight, I'm going to get…a double scoop of strawberry mixed with white chocolate chips.

pistashio
(pih-STASH-ee-o)
A tasty nut with a greenish color used in ice cream and in baking.

In a cup—not a cone—because it's so hot outside and I don't want it to drip."

While Troy shook his head in amazement, Dad stepped up and ordered his royal peach ice cream—in a cone, because, as he told everyone, *he* was going to eat it before it had time to melt.

Becky ordered a caramel milkshake with extra caramel drizzle, and Sam asked for a double scoop of chocolate chip cookie dough ice cream with chocolate sprinkles in a sugar cone. Mr. and Mrs. Jamison and Mom all got raspberry sherbet, and Mrs. Jamison ordered a kid's cup of chocolate-vanilla swirl for Eden.

"What about you, Troy?" asked Andrew. "Are you going to get your usual?"

"No," Troy said as he stepped up to give his order. "I'm going to be wild and crazy like you and get something totally different."

Troy raised his chin and gave the girl behind the counter his order. "Two scoops of vanilla in a regular cone, please."

He didn't understand why everyone was laughing.

Chapter 13
Who?

"Hey, Troy," whispered Sam across the picnic table where everyone sat eating their ice cream. "Do you think that's L.C.? Mrs. Ellis said she worked at the putt-putt. Maybe her job is scooping ice cream."

"I can't see her name tag. Ask Becky."

"Becky," hissed Sam. "Is that girl's name L.C.?"

"How would I know?"

"Look at her name tag, silly. Is it L.C.?"

"I can't tell. She's moving around too much. Ask Mom."

"Hey, Mom," said Sam, "can you see the name of the girl scooping ice cream?"

"No, I can't see her name tag. Maybe Ed knows who she is."

"Mr. Jamison? Do you know the name of the girl that's working at the ice cream counter?"

"You mean L.C.? Sure, I know her. She's a great girl. Her real name is Lila Cunningham. She works at the library and here at the putt-putt. She works over in Southport too sometimes. She's saving money to go to college next year."

Sam turned back to tell the others what he had found. "That is L.C., but listen to this: her real name is Lila Cunningham."

Sam looked meaningfully at Troy and Becky. "Don't you get it? Her real name is Lila Cunningham."

Sam raised his eyebrows so high that Becky started laughing.

"So what, Sam?" she said. "So her name is Lila. So what?"

"Her name," said Sam again, but this time *very* slowly, "is Lila C."

He sighed when Becky and Troy just looked at him with puzzled looks. He turned over the little card where he had written down everyone's score during the miniature golf game. With the little yellow pencil, he wrote:

LILA C

"Oh, right," said Troy smiling and nodding at last. "She works at the library and her name is LILA C."

Chapter 14
Take a Message

After they finished their ice cream, Troy, Sam, Becky, and Andrew went over to talk to the girl behind the counter.

"Your name's Lila, right?" asked Troy.

"Yes it is, but everyone calls me L.C. Hi, Andrew."

"Hi," said Andrew.

"You know L.C.?" Troy asked Andrew.

"Sure. I met her at the library. I go there a lot, remember?"

"Mrs. Ellis over at the library said you were an expert on Stede Bonnet," said Sam.

"I should say I am! I've been reading stories about Stede Bonnet since the summer I graduated from fifth grade."

L.C. **propped** her elbows on the ice cream counter and held her face in her hands. "Why are you all so interested in Stede Bonnet?"

Troy looked at Sam, Sam looked at Becky, and Becky looked at Andrew, but Andrew just shrugged his shoulders.

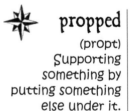 **propped**
(propt)
Supporting something by putting something else under it.

"We think he sent us a message!" Troy blurted out. "Actually a couple of messages."

L.C.'s mouth fell open. She looked like she'd seen a ghost. "You think *Stede Bonnet* sent you messages? You know he's dead, right? He's been dead a long time. You know that, right?"

"Yes."

"But you think he sent you messages?"

"Somebody sent them. We're just not sure who," Sam said.

"But you think it might be Stede Bonnet?"

"Yes."

"Can I see the messages?"

"No."

"Why not?"

"We don't have them with us," said Troy.

"That's because one was written in the bushes below the lighthouse," clarified Becky.

L.C. wrinkled her forehead like she was listening to a language she didn't understand. She was just about to pepper them with questions when Mr. Jamison came up to the counter.

"Hi, L.C.," said Mr. Jamison, resting his hands on Troy's and Andrew's shoulders. "I *thought* that was you up there dishing out the ice cream. You looked pretty busy so I didn't want to bother you. I see you've met my two boys and their friends here. How's that little car of yours running?"

"It gets me around, Mr. Jamison. I got it painted, so now it's a nice, bright red. Wolf Pack red, I think they called it.

"Oh, that's too bad, L.C. I'm so sorry." Mr. Jamison shook his head. "Didn't they have any of that nice Carolina blue paint?"

"They were all out, sir. Such a shame." L.C. pretended to shake her head sadly, but then she grinned. "I think red is a much better color for me—considering where I'm going to school in the fall."

Mr. Jamison laughed. "Hey, can you come out for dinner tomorrow night? There's a turtle nest in front of the house that hatched last night and the turtle folks are checking the nest for stragglers tomorrow evening. We'll get a chance to show our California friends how we take care of our sea turtles."

"Thanks, Mr. Jamison, I'd love to. How about if I bring my Grandma Terry's famous key lime pie?"

"Perfect!" said Mr. Jamison. "We'll see you then."

"That sounds great!" Becky said with a quick glance at Sam, Troy, and Andrew.

vigorously
(VIG-or-us-lee)
With lots of energy and excitement.

"Then we'll have a chance to tell L.C. what we saw at the lighthouse."

L.C. raised her eyebrows as the boys nodded **vigorously** in agreement.

Chapter 15
Come for Dinner

Tonight there was a full moon.

Tonight, the sea turtle people were checking the turtle nest right at the end of the beach house boardwalk.

And tonight, Mr. and Mrs. Jamison were fixing a special dinner—a traditional North Carolina low country boil—for everyone at the house plus a few guests, including L.C.

A low-country boil, Mr. Jamison had explained to Dad, is a great way to feed a lot of people. The name came from the coastal plains of North and South Carolina, an area known as the low country. A low country

crab crackers

(krab KRAK-urz) Also known as nut crackers, this handy tool lets you crack open the hard shell of the crab—especially the crab claws—so you can get all of the delicious meat inside!

boil included all kinds of seafood, like shrimp, mussels, clams, and crabs along with potatoes, onions, sausage, and corn on the cob. Everything cooked in the same big pot along with some Old Bay seasoning.

"Yum, YUM!" said Mr. Jamison as he rubbed his hands and smiled. "I guarantee you'll love it!"

While the food cooked, Mom and Mrs. Jamison spread lots of newspapers on the table. They put out rolls of paper towels to use as napkins and stacks of plates. Forks, knives, and **crab crackers** were in a bucket in the middle of each table beside glasses of ice and huge pitchers of sweet tea.

"Here we go," said Mr. Jamison as he and Dad brought platters of food out for everyone to eat. "It's already been blessed, so go ahead and help yourself."

*****

"I'm stuffed," said Sam.

"I didn't think I'd ever hear those words from Sam's mouth," Mom said to Mrs. Jamison with a laugh. "These days, Sam eats enough for about three boys his size."

"I know what you mean," said Mrs. Jamison. "Try multiplying that by two!"

"Is there anything else we can do to help clean up, Mrs. Jamison?" asked Becky.

"No thanks, sweetie. Ed and your father said they would finish all the dishes. It helps a lot when all you have to do is roll up the newspaper tablecloth and throw it away. We're pretty much done."

"There's a tiny piece of key lime pie left," called Dad from the kitchen. "Unless anyone else wants it, I'll…"

But nobody could understand the rest of Dad's words because he had a mouth full of pie!

"When are the turtle people checking the nest that hatched?" asked Sam.

"Not until it gets a little darker and you can see the moon better." said Mrs. Jamison. "Any baby turtles that are still in the nest need to follow the path of the moon to the ocean."

"What about when there's no moon?" asked Becky.

"Then the turtle folks use their flashlights to guide the baby turtles to the water," said L.C.

"Why don't they just pick up the turtles and put them in the ocean?" asked Sam.

"Because," Mrs. Jamison said, "it's very important that the baby turtles do it for themselves. It helps them get ready for their dive into the big, dangerous world. It's not easy being a little sea turtle. Not many of them grow up to be adults. That's why they're an endangered species."

"Luckily there's a full moon tonight," said L.C., "but it won't be dark enough to check the turtles for another hour or so."

"Sounds like we have time for a walk on the beach," said Troy with a grin. "Come on, L.C."

Chapter 16
In the Sand

Although it was still early in the evening, the full moon was already making a moon path on the patient ocean waves.

Troy, Andrew, Sam, and Becky walked down the beach with L.C.—all of them telling her about the mysterious messages at the same time.

"When we went to the top of the lighthouse," started Troy, "we saw a message in the bushes. Right…about…here.

"From the top of the lighthouse it looked like the message said *SOS*," said Troy.

"Then, when Troy's mom bought him a journal in Southport, a piece of paper dropped out of it and it had a puzzle on the back," continued Becky.

"It turned out to be a code, and when we finally figured it out, it looked like this." Andrew wrote the message in the sand.

LILAC AT THE LIBRARY B4 FULL MOON.

Sam took up the story. "Then we figured out that the message really said LILA C not LILAC and we found you."

"But the thing that started everything," said Becky, "was two nights ago when, instead of flashing four flashes, the lighthouse beam…"

"…flashed three," finished L.C.

"You saw that too?" asked Sam, in surprise.

"I did. I thought maybe I'd made a mistake in counting the flashes."

"But you didn't, did you?" said Troy. "I thought I'd made a mistake too, until I talked with Sam and Becky."

"What do you think it means?" asked Becky.

"Well, it *does* seems like somebody wanted to get all of us together," said L.C.

"But why?" asked Becky.

"Do you think it's Stede Bonnet who wants us all together?" asked Sam.

"I don't know," said L.C. "It could be… after all, I am his great, great, great, great, great, great, great, great, great, great-granddaughter."

Speechless, Sam, Becky, Troy, and Andrew just stared at L.C.

Finally Andrew said, "You're Stede Bonnet's great, great, great-granddaughter?"

"Seven more *greats*, but yes, I am."

"So *that's* why you're such an expert."

"Yeah, it's a family thing. The story is that one of Stede Bonnet's daughters got married and moved up here after he died. We don't know exactly why she moved here, although some people think she was trying to get away from her mother."

"But what would Stede Bonnet want from you after all these years?" asked Becky.

"And why would he want all of us together?" Andrew wrinkled his forehead.

"I don't know," said L.C. "It doesn't make any sense to me."

Everyone was quiet for a moment trying to figure out what Stede Bonnet could possibly want from them. The only sound was the crashing and sighing of the waves as they moved up and back on the shore.

"This is crazy!" said Troy. "I just want to yell out, 'Found her!' or write it here on the beach." He traced the words in the sand with his big toe.

"Maybe we should use the bushes and vines to send a message back—you know, like the one we saw from the top of the lighthouse," said Sam.

"Guys?" said Becky.

"That would be really hard to do," Andrew said. "Besides, I don't think the people around here would like us cutting down the bushes and making messages out of the vines."

"Guys…" said Becky a little louder.

"We could write a message on the back of the Pirate Days flyer, put it in a bottle, and throw it into the ocean," Troy offered.

"GUYS!" said Becky, "Look!"

"What, Becky?" said Sam crossly. "So you wrote *THANKS* in the sand. What's the big deal? Why did you write that?"

"I didn't."

"What do you mean?"

"I didn't write it. Watch."

✦ sarcastically
(sar-KASS-tick-lee)
Saying the opposite of what you mean with the purpose of making someone feel bad. Nice, huh?

They all watched as a wave washed away the word that had been so neatly written in the sand.

"That's great, Becky," said Sam **sarcastically**. "Isn't that what usually happens when a wave…"

126

Sam stopped talking, and—with everyone else—watched silently as the word *THANKS* was slowly rewritten on the sand. At the end of the sand writing were two letters written very close together.

Nobody said a word, but they all watched as another wave washed away the writing.

And they kept watching as someone…or something… rewrote the same message in the sand a third time.

After a wave washed it away a third time, the message did not come back.

"It's a message from Stede Bonnet," said Sam. "It has to be. Those are his initials: *S* and *B*."

127

"Oh my gosh," whispered L.C. "You're right! It is an *S*. I've seen these initials before in my grandmother's house, but I always thought it was a *G* and a *B*. Her name is Grace Bradley."

"Where did you see the initials?" asked Andrew.

"That's what I can't remember. I know I've seen them *somewhere*." L.C. bent down to draw Stede Bonnet's initials in the sand. "S and B. Why didn't I think about that?"

"Do you think Stede Bonnet wrote back to us because Troy wrote him a note in the sand?" asked Andrew.

"Maybe…" L.C. was thoughtful.

"Because if he did," continued Andrew, "then we could write another message and ask what he wants."

"That's brilliant, Andrew" said Troy. "We could…"

"Wait a minute," said Becky. "There's Dad and Mr. Jamison waving at us. It must be time to check on the sea turtles."

"Let's come back here after the sea turtles are all taken care of," suggested Troy. "Then we can find out what Mr. Stede Bonnet wants."

Great idea, Troy!" said Sam. "I'll race you guys. Ready, set, go!"

And with that, Sam was off, running down the beach with Becky, Andrew, L.C., and Troy right behind him.

129

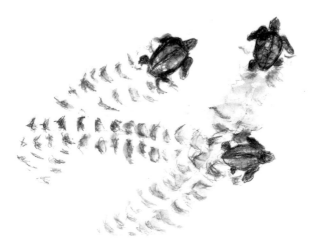

Chapter 17
The Last Word

When the sea turtle people came to check the turtle nest, they found that 11 more sea turtles had hatched! The turtle people made a smooth path on the sand from the nest to the waves, and then—one by one—they put the baby turtles onto the moon path that would lead them to their new home in the ocean.

On the sidelines, Oak Island visitors and residents alike watched with delight, cheering for the tiny turtles as they scrambled toward the surf.

Whenever a little turtle went the wrong way or got stuck in a track made by a brother or sister, the crowd offered encouragement to the newly hatched baby.

"No flash pictures, please," the turtle man reminded the onlookers. "The baby turtles get confused if they see extra lights and they can end up crawling in the wrong direction. That's another reason this species is endangered. The lights we humans use—everything from porch lights to the lighthouse itself—make it difficult for the baby turtles to get to the ocean. There are lots of predators on the island who would love to have one of these little guys for dinner."

After the last little turtle made its way into the waves, the crowd drifted apart. Some people returned to their houses, and some walked down the beach toward the pier. But Sam, Becky, Andrew, Troy, and L.C. headed back up the beach toward the lighthouse.

The sky was dark when they reached the lighthouse, and the moon was setting over the ocean.

"I have a great book about sea turtles," said Andrew. "I wish I'd brought it. I was reading it right before we left and I forgot to bring it. It's probably still sitting on that old trunk in my bedroom. I can't believe—"

"That's it!" said L.C. suddenly. "The old trunk! That's where I saw the initials."

"You mean Stede Bonnet's initials?" asked Becky.

"Yes! I saw them on top of an old trunk in my grandmother's attic. It was the first year I came to Oak Island. I had just finished fifth grade, and my parents let me spend the whole summer down here. I loved it!

"One rainy day I was exploring in Grandmama's attic and I saw the trunk. I remember thinking how cool it was that her initials were on the top. But then I found some old **Nancy Drew** books, so I took them downstairs and started to read. I never thought about that trunk again…until now."

"Is the trunk still there?" asked Troy.

✳ Nancy Drew

(NAN-see Drew)
A series of popular mystery books by Carolyn Keene—first printed in 1930—and featuring a girl detective as the main character. (I loved Nancy Drew books when I was growing up!)

"Yes!" said L.C. "I saw it just the other day when I took some things up to the attic for my grandmother."

Then she groaned. "Oh no, I forgot. Grandmama is out of town for the next two days. She always keeps the attic locked and she has the only key. We can't find out what's in the trunk until then."

"After tonight, the moon won't be full again for a whole month and we'll be gone by then," pointed out Becky.

Everyone was quiet, trying to think of a way to find out what was in the trunk.

"Why don't we ask Stede Bonnet?" said Sam.

They all looked at Sam and then they looked at each other. Then they all grinned.

"Who's going to write the message?" asked Troy.

"I vote for L.C. to write it," said Andrew. "After all, finding L.C. is what Stede Bonnet wanted us to do, right?"

"Right, and she is his great, great…great, great, great—oh, you know what I mean—granddaughter," added Troy.

"Okay," said L.C., "I'll write the message. Here goes." Using a stick for her pencil, L.C. wrote in the sand:

What is in the trunk?

She and the others watched the sand as words slowly appeared—written by an invisible hand, right before their eyes.

Tis my greatest treasure

Whoops and cheers went up from L.C., Sam, Becky, Andrew, and Troy.

"Ask him what he wants us to do, or how we can help," said Andrew excitedly.

L.C. wrote the question in the sand:

How can we help?

Everyone held their breath, waiting…

"He's writing something!" cried Andrew.

The words appeared slowly.

Beware of Bla...

But then the writing stopped—right in the middle of the word. And when a wave washed over the message and erased it, the words didn't come back.

"What's wrong?" said Troy. "Did something happen?"

"Why did he stop writing?" asked Becky.

"He was trying to tell us something," said L.C.

"He was trying to *warn* us about something," said Troy. "The message said 'Beware of Bla…"

"He was telling us to watch out for Blackbeard, don't you think?" asked Sam. "The question is why did he stop writing?"

"I bet it's the moon," said Andrew looking out over the ocean. "I bet the sand writing only works when there's a full moon—that's why we had to find L.C. so quickly. The moon was full tonight, but it just set."

Everyone turned to look to the western horizon. Sure enough, there was no more silvery path on the ocean. The big, full moon had set and the path had vanished.

The beam from the lighthouse seemed even brighter in the dark night.

******

"*When* is your grandmother coming back?" asked Sam.

"Grandmama won't be back until the day after tomorrow, but as soon as she gets back we can open the trunk **A.S.A.P.** "

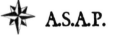 **A.S.A.P.**
An abbreviation for as soon as possible.

L.C. smiled. "Maybe the Southport museum will want the trunk. Maybe they'll do an exhibit all about Stede Bonnet—wouldn't that be cool?"

"Will you tell them about the sand writing?" Troy asked.

"I don't know," said L.C. "Maybe... someday. But not right now."

She rubbed her toe in the sand, drawing an *S* and a *B*. "You know...I can't ever thank you guys enough," she said very quietly. "I was wondering how I was going to pay for college next year."

"You never know," said Andrew. "The trunk may not have anything in it at all. But if it's been in your grandmother's house all this time..."

"Just make sure you let us know when you're going to open it, okay?" said Troy. He was hanging back a little, walking behind everyone else.

"I promise," said L.C. "You'll all be the very first to know!"

*****

Troy turned around to watch the beam from the Oak Island Lighthouse flash across the sand and over the water.

One-two-three-four-off. Everything was just as it should be.

He jogged to catch up with the others, and then he joined in on the conversation as they talked fast and walked slowly down the beach and away from the lighthouse.

The lighthouse beam continued to shine it's beam across the sand and over the water.

One-two-three-four-off.

One-two-three-four-off.

One-two-three-off...

Chapter 18
What's Next?

"We drive the car right onto the boat? We've been on ferries in California," Sam said, "but we just walk onto them. This is *so* cool!"

Sam, Becky, Troy, Andrew, and their families were on their way to the North Carolina Aquarium at Fort Fisher. The fastest way to get there (and definitely the most fun) was to ride the ferry across the Cape Fear River.

"I like that you can see the Bald Head Lighthouse *and* the Oak Island Lighthouse from here," said Troy.

Actually, son," said a gruff voice behind them, "if ye wait a minute, ye'll be able to see a third lighthouse. One that most people forget about—though they ought not."

knapsack
(NAP-sac)
A backpack made out of cloth that has flaps instead of zippers and is used to carry supplies.

Troy, Sam, Becky, and Andrew turned around to see an old man in saggy jeans and a wrinkled blue shirt. He had a red bandana tied around his long gray hair, a bushy beard, and a small gold ring in his ear. He carried a dark green **knapsack** over his shoulder.

"Aye, lighthouses always give direction of some sort," the old man continued. "You just have to know how to read them. It's like they say,

Watch the flash, mind the light,
Heed the warning beam so bright.
Through darkest night
and stormy seas
They light the way and bring ye peace.

Becky raised her eyebrows and traded looks with Andrew, Sam, and Troy.

"Old Stede Bonnet sure knew the value of a lighthouse. There she is." The old man pointed toward the shoreline.

"Price's Creek Lighthouse is one of the most helpful lighthouses you'll ever see."

Sam, Becky, Troy, and Andrew turned back to look toward the shore where the man pointed. All they could see was a small brick tower in a swamp.

"Is that stack of bricks the Price's Creek Lighthouse?" asked Sam.

When the man didn't answer, Sam turned around, but there was no one there.

"Where did he go?" asked Sam.

"Did he fall in the water?" Andrew peered over the edge of the ferry, but saw only seagulls.

"That's just weird," said Becky looking around. "People don't just disappear like that."

"Did you guys notice that man's hair?" asked Troy. "Under that bandana, it was totally gray—almost white."

"He was an old guy, Troy," said Andrew. "What did you expect? What I want to know is where did he go?"

"His hair was gray," said Troy slowly, "but his beard didn't have a speck of white in it. He had a totally black beard."

Sam, Andrew, and Becky looked at Troy and then at each other with big, round eyes. But they said absolutely nothing.

THE END

Have Fun and Learn More

Remember I said there were lots of great books to read and web sites to visit? Well, here are some of my favorites.

Books to Read

Katherine L. House. *Lighthouses for Kids*. Chicago: Chicago Review Press, Inc., 2008.

Wechter, Nell Wise and Bland Simpson. *Taffy of Torpedo Junction*. Chapel Hill, NC: Chapel Hill Books, 1957.

Zepke, Terrance. *Lighthouses of the Carolinas for Kids*. Sarasota, Florida: Pineapple Press, Inc., 2009.

Web Sites to Visit

Lighthouses of the United States: North Carolina. Russ Rowlett. September 1999. University of North Carolina at Chapel Hill. November 2012. <www.unc.edu/~rowlett/ lighthouse/nc.htm>

North Carolina Coastal Adventures. Melissa Carle and Jennifer Rouse. 2006. North Carolina Division of Coastal Management, Department of Environment and Natural Resources. November 2012. <dcm2.enr.state.nc.us/wetlands/coastal_ explorers/cpfmodule/cpf_animals.htm>

Oak Island Lighthouse. 2012. Friends of Oak Island Lighthouse. November 2012. <www.oakislandlighthouse.org>

"Oak Island, NC." *LighthouseFriends. com.* 2001. LighthouseFriends.com. November 2012. <www.lighthousefriends. com/light.asp?ID=352>

Coming Soon from

A&M Writing and Publishing

The Clue at Price's Creek

Tag along with Sam, Becky, Andrew, and Troy as they explore the Cape Fear River and try to find a clue in the ruins of a lighthouse that's in a swamp and off limits to the public!

Is the mystery at an end, or can they help their friend L.C. figure out the strange request from her great, great grandfather?

A&M Writing and Publishing, Santa Clara, California
www.amwriting.com

MICHIGAN LIGHTHOUSE ADVENTURES

Join Sam and Becky in their very first lighthouse adventure on Michigan's amazing Upper Peninsula!

- **THE CLUE AT COPPER HARBOR**
- **THE MYSTERY AT EAGLE HARBORR**
- **THE SECRET OF BETE GRISE BAY**

Published by A&M Writing and Publishing, Santa Clara, California
www.amwriting.com

INTRODUCTION

You should find *Access 2002 From A to Z* easy to use. To use the book, you only need to know that the book organizes its information — the tasks and important terms — alphabetically in order from A to Z (rather like an index). The book also has an index in the back, to make it even easier to fine what you need.

You'll find it helpful, however, if you understand what this book assumes about your computer skills, what you should know about the Access program from the very start, and what editorial conventions this book uses. This short introduction provides this information.

What You Should Know About Windows

You don't need to be a computer expert to use either this book or Microsoft Access. But you want to be comfortable working with your computer and Microsoft Windows.

For example, you should know how to turn your computer on and off, how to start and stop programs, how to choose menu commands, and how to work with dialog boxes. This book, for the most part, doesn't provide this Windows information.

If you need this Windows information, you need to take the Windows on-line tutorial, get a friend to give you a quick tutorial, or acquire another book on Windows.

TIP *Any short book on Windows will tell you what you need to know, but if you're a business user of Windows 2000 or Windows XP, you may want to look at the* Effective Executive's Guide to Windows 2000 *or the* Effective Executive's Guide to Windows XP. *These books supply a tutorial on Windows geared for business professionals.*

What You Should Know About Access

If you are familiar with other Microsoft programs, such as Word and Excel, you need to understand that Access works a bit differently. Some things, such as toolbars, maximize and minimize buttons, and menu commands, work exactly the same; but Access doesn't produce separate files the way that Word produces documents and Excel produces workbooks.

An Access database is one single file that contains many database *objects*. Objects include:

- *tables* (where all the data is stored)
- *forms* (for entering, editing, and viewing data one record at a time)
- *reports* (printable pages of organized, summarized data)
- *queries* (specific sets of data retrieved, or queried, from tables)
- *macros* and *modules* (for automating database actions)
- *data access pages* (for posting database objects on a web page)

TIP   *Always remember that ALL database data is stored in the tables. Queries, forms, and reports are just different means of working with the data in the tables—they don't contain any data themselves.*

The easiest way to open an existing Access database is to choose the File→Open command, navigate to the location of the database file, and double-click the name of the file to open it.

NOTE   *When you open Access, the Access program window opens with a task pane on the right side. In Access, the task pane is redundant and tends to confuse things—you can close the task pane by clicking the X in its upper-right corner. If you need the task pane, you can open it by choosing the File→New command.*

When you open an Access database, the database file is represented by the database window, as shown in Figure 1. Although the database window can be maximized, it's more efficient to work with the database window in an intermediate size.

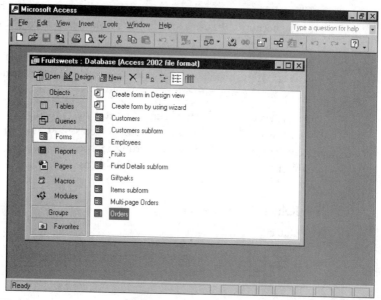

Figure 1 A database window in the Access window.

On the left side of the database window is the *Objects bar*. In the Objects bar are the names of object groups. If you want to see a list of all the forms in the database, for example, click Forms in the Objects bar. All the forms are listed in the main database window pane (as shown in Figure 1).

To open a specific object, such as a particular table, show the list of tables in the database window and then double-click the name of the table you want to open.

What You Should Know About This Book

You already know the most important feature of this book — that it organizes its task descriptions and term definitions alphabetically. But let me comment quickly on two other important conventions.

- When this book refers to some box or button label, the label description appears in all initial capital letters. So, while the Font dialog box includes a check box labeled "Double strikethrough," this book would refer to the Double Strikethrough check box. The initial capital letters, then, signal you that the book refers to an on-screen label.

- This book's pictures of windows and dialog boxes may look a bit funny to you because they use a low display resolution to make the buttons, boxes, and text look larger. Less information fits on the screen when the resolution is low, unfortunately, but what you see on the book's pages, you can read. If the book's screen pictures had used a higher resolution, images would be very difficult to see clearly.

And that's everything you should know to get started. Good luck. Be patient in your learning. Have fun with Microsoft Access 2002. It's an amazing program, and you may find yourself getting hooked on it. Be sure to read the Troubleshooting entry if you encounter problems.

Julia Kelly and Steve Nelson
May 2001

ACCESS 2002 FROM A TO Z

& (Ampersand) see Concatenate

Access Project

An Access project is a file that's a collection of Access database objects (forms, reports, data access pages, and so forth) that get their data from an external SQL Server database. An Access project doesn't contain any data, tables, or relationships of its own. The database objects in an Access project are created in exactly the same way as regular Access database objects. When your database's data load becomes too large for Access to handle efficiently, you'll want to move your data to a SQL Server database and use an Access project to enter, edit, and retrieve the data stored there.

SEE ALSO *SQL Server*

Aligning Controls see Controls

Aligning Text in Controls

To align the characters in a control, open the form or report in Design view and select the control. Use the Align Left, Center, and Align Right buttons on the Formatting toolbar to align the control's characters the way you want them.

Ampersand (&) see Concatenate

AND Filter

An AND filter is a filter that finds records that meet one criterion AND another. It might look for records that have a criterion in one field AND a criterion in another field, or for records that have one criterion AND another in the same field. An example of an AND filter is one that filters a Products table for a particular product AND a price range.

SEE ALSO *Filters*

Arguments see Functions, Macros

Ask A Question Box

The Ask A Question box is a much less intrusive form of the Office Assistant. It's the box that sits in the upper-right corner of your program window (shown in Figure A-1). To use it, type a word or phrase in the box, and press Enter. Then click a topic on the help topics menu that drops open. The help window opens at that point, and you can search more deeply for help with your question.

Figure A-1   The Ask A Question box.

SEE ALSO *Help*

AutoCorrect

AutoCorrect fixes common typing mistakes. Access already knows about many of the typing mistakes that people commonly make. For example, Access knows how to correctly capitalize the first letter of a sentence and how to spell commonly misspelled words.

You don't need to do anything special to use AutoCorrect. Access's corrections of your spelling and typing mistakes will occur automatically. If AutoCorrect makes a change you don't want, press Ctrl+Z immediately to undo the change and return to what you typed.

NOTE   *To change the way that AutoCorrect works, choose the Tools→AutoCorrect Options command. When Access displays the AutoCorrect dialog box, use it to set up how AutoCorrect should operate.*

AutoExec Macro

AutoExec is a macro name that Access recognizes. Access runs the AutoExec macro automatically when the database opens (the AutoExec macro is commonly used to open a switchboard form when a database opens).

To create an AutoExec macro, create the macro action you want to run when the database opens—for example, create a macro that uses the OpenForm action to open a specific form—and when you save the macro, name it **AutoExec**.

TIP   *To open a database without running its AutoExec macro, hold down the Shift key while you open the database.*

SEE ALSO *Macros, Switchboard*

AutoForm

An AutoForm is a form that's created automatically by the Form Wizard, with no user input. To create an AutoForm, click the name of the table or query (in the database window) for which you want a form. On the Access toolbar, click the arrow next to the New Object button, and click AutoForm.

SEE ALSO *Forms*

AutoKeys

AutoKeys is a macro name that Access recognizes. AutoKeys macros attach macro actions to keystrokes. For example, you can create an AutoKeys macro that opens a particular form when you press Ctrl+Y. All AutoKeys macros are kept in a single macro group that's named AutoKeys.

To create an AutoKeys macro, open a new macro window, then click View→Macro Names to show the Macro Name column.

In the Macro Name column, type the keystrokes for the macro (use the caret (^) symbol for Ctrl, and the plus (+) symbol for Shift). In the Action column, select a macro action, and fill in the macro arguments in the Action Arguments pane.

Save the macro with the name AutoKeys. If you create more AutoKeys macros, open the existing AutoKeys macro in Design view, and add them to the list.

SEE ALSO *Macros*

AutoNumber

AutoNumber is a field data type that automatically stores a unique number for each record that is added to a table. Numbers generated by an AutoNumber field can't be changed or replaced. AutoNumber is the data type that the Table Wizard assigns to an ID field when you allow the wizard to create a primary key for you. You can also assign AutoNumber to an ID field yourself when you create a new table without using the wizard.

To assign the AutoNumber data type to a field, open the table in Design view. In the Data Type column for that field, select AutoNumber.

NOTE   *When creating table relationships, a field with the AutoNumber data type matches a field with a Number data type and Long Integer size.*

SEE ALSO   *Data Types*

AutoReport

An AutoReport is a report that's created automatically by the Report Wizard, with no user input. To create an AutoReport, click the name of the table or query (in the database window) for which you want a report. On the Access toolbar, click the arrow next to the New Object button, and click AutoReport.

SEE ALSO   *Report*

Background Pictures

Forms and reports can have background pictures as part of the overall formatting of the object. Many of the styles offered by the Form Wizard are made colorful by their background pictures. You can add your own background pictures to forms and reports.

NOTE   *Background pictures are visually appealing, but they can make a form or report very difficult to read; so use them sparingly if at all.*

Background Pictures in Forms

To add a background picture to a form:

1. Open the form in Design view.

2. Right-click on the gray square in the upper-left corner of the form, and click Properties on the shortcut menu.

3. In the Form properties sheet that opens, on the Format tab, scroll down to the Picture property and click in the box (shown in Figure B-1).

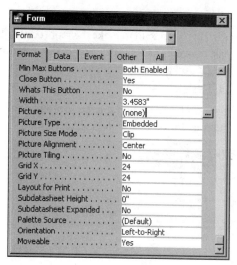

Figure B-1   The Picture property on the Format tab of the Form properties sheet.

4. A button with three dots appears—click the button to open the Insert Picture dialog box.

5. Navigate to the picture file you want to use, and double-click the picture's file name.

The picture is placed in the form's background, and the path to the picture appears in the Picture property box.

- You can alter the picture's appearance by changing the Picture Size Mode property: Clip crops a large picture down to fit in the form, Stretch resizes the entire picture to fit in the form, and Zoom makes the picture grow or shrink to maintain its original proportions while filling the form.

- While the Properties sheet is open, you can also tell Access where to position the picture in the form, by selecting a position in the Picture Alignment property.

To remove a picture from the background of a form, follow steps 1 through 3 above to open the Picture property for the form, and delete the entry in the Picture property.

To change the color of a form's background (without adding a picture), open the form in Design view, then right-click the form grid and click Properties. On the Format tab, click in the Back Color property, and click the button with three dots that appears. Click a new color in the Color dialog box.

Background Pictures in Reports

Pictures in a report's background tend to make the report difficult to read, but if a picture is in pale colors or shades of pale gray (like a watermark), they can be effective. To add a background picture to a report:

1. Open the report in Design view.

2. Right-click on the gray square in the upper-left corner of the report (shown in Figure B-2), and click Properties on the shortcut menu.

Figure B-2   The gray square that opens the report's Properties sheet.

3. In the Report properties sheet that opens, on the Format tab, scroll down to the Picture property and click in the box.

4. A button with three dots appears—click the button to open the Insert Picture dialog box.

5. Navigate to the picture file you want to use, and double-click the picture's file name.

The picture is placed in the report's background, and the path to the picture appears in the Picture property box.

- You can alter the picture's appearance by changing the Picture Size Mode property. Clip crops a large picture down to fit in the form, Stretch resizes the entire picture to fit in the form, and Zoom makes the picture grow or shrink to maintain its original proportions while filling the form.

- While the Properties sheet is open, you can also tell Access where to position the picture in the report, by selecting a position in the Picture Alignment property.

- In a report, you can choose to show the picture on all the report pages, or only on the first page. Make that selection in the Picture Pages property.

To remove a picture from the background of a form, follow steps 1 through 3 above to open the Picture property for the report, and delete the entry in the Picture property.

Backups

When you've gathered lots of data or created terrific forms and reports, it's a shame to lose them to a computer malfunction. To back up your data or any of the objects in your database, export the objects to another database or to another file type.

SEE ALSO *Exporting Data*

Borders see Formatting Controls

Bound Control

A bound control is a control that's tied to a specific field in a query or table, and displays the data in that field. For example, a text box in a form that displays a customer's last name is a control that's bound to the last name field in the underlying table.

SEE ALSO *Controls*

Bound Object Frame

A bound object frame is a control that displays objects (usually graphic objects) that are stored in a table field; a bound object frame displays a specific object for each record in the table.

To store graphic objects in the records of a table (for example, pictures of products or employees), create a field in the table and give the field a data type of OLE Object. Save the table, and in Datasheet view, right-click in the cell where you want to enter the graphic object.

In the shortcut menu, click Insert Object. Click the Create From File option, and click the Browse button, navigate to the picture file, and double-click the file name. This enters the graphic object in a specific record in the table.

NOTE   *The picture won't appear in the table, but the path to the picture will appear, and the picture will appear in the bound object frame in forms and reports.*

To see the picture in a report or form, add a bound object frame control to the form or report. When the form or report displays each record, the graphic object inserted in the record will be displayed.

SEE ALSO *Controls*

Calculated Controls

A calculated control is a control (usually a text box) that is not bound to any particular field of data—instead, it contains an expression that calculates values.

To create a calculated control in a form or report, create an unbound text box in the form: in the Toolbox, click on the Text Box button, then click in the form grid or report page.

To create a calculated expression in the unbound control, do one of these two things:

- Type the expression in the text box.
- Right-click in the text box and click Properties. On the Data tab, click in the Control Source property, and click the Build button (the button with three dots). Use the Expression Builder to build your calculation expression.

NOTE   *If you want to type the expression yourself, but need more room, open the Properties sheet for the control and click in the Control Source property on the Data tab. Then press Shift + F2 to open a Zoom box, where you have lots of room to type your expression.*

NOTE   *If you create a calculated control to sum the details in a report's grouping, be sure you put the calculated control in the group's header or footer, not in the group's Detail section. To show a header or footer for a particular field group, choose the View→Sorting And Grouping command, and click in the Field/ Expression name in the Sorting And Grouping dialog box. Then, under Group Properties, select Yes in the Group Header or Group Footer box.*

SEE ALSO *Expression*

Calculated Field

A calculated field is a query field that contains an expression that performs calculations on the values in other fields in the query. For example, if an orders query shows fields for Quantity and for Price, another field in the query (a calculated field) can use an expression to multiply the value in the Quantity field by the value in the Price field, to display a total. An expression that multiplies a field named Quantity by a field named Price looks like this: **Expr1: [Quantity]*[Price]** (shown in Figure C-1). Field names are enclosed in square brackets.

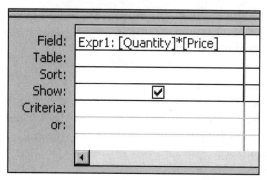

Figure C-1 A calculated field in a query QBE grid.

NOTE   *The Expr1 portion of the expression is a caption that appears in the column heading in Datasheet view. You can replace the Expr1 characters with your own caption for the calculated field.*

Captions

A caption is the field column heading that's displayed in Datasheet view; it doesn't have to be identical to the field name. Access identifies the field by its field name (and the field name is used in calculations, relationships, macros, and other database activities), but a caption displayed to users, and can be much more friendly or intuitive than the field name.

To create or change a field caption in a table, open the table in Design view. Click in the field row in the upper pane, and then type or edit the caption in the Caption property in the Field Properties pane.

To create or change a field caption in a query, open the query in Design view. In the Field row for the field that you want to change, type the caption and a colon on the left side of the field name or expression (as shown in Figure C-2).

Figure C-2 The caption for this calculated query field is **Name**.

Cascade Deletes and Updates

If referential integrity is enforced in a table relationship, you cannot delete or update a record from the primary side of a table relationship unless Cascade Deletes and Cascade Updates are allowed. If Cascade Deletes are allowed, when you delete a record from the primary table, the related records in the related table are automatically deleted as well (although Access warns you before deleting the related records). If Cascade Updates are allowed, when you change a primary key value from the primary table, the related values in the related table are automatically updated with the change.

To set or change the Cascade settings in a relationship, open the Relationships window and show the two related tables. Right-click the join line between the tables and click Edit Relationship. Mark the Cascade Delete Related Records check box (shown in Figure C-3) to allow primary record deletion with automatic related record deletion. Mark the Cascade Update Related Fields check box to allow primary key value changes with automatic updating of related values.

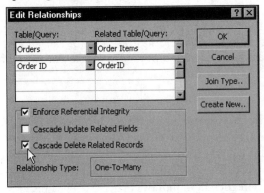

Figure C-3   If the Enforce Referential Integrity check box is marked, you can mark the Cascade check boxes.

SEE ALSO *Primary Key, Referential Integrity*

Cell

A cell is the intersection of a row and a column in Datasheet view.

Charts

You can chart Access data either by using the Access Chart Wizard or by sending your data to Excel and using Excel's Chart Wizard. The Access Chart Wizard creates a report with a chart on it which is difficult to customize and not very flexible. Excel's Chart Wizard, on the other hand, is a much more creative and flexible chart engine, and vastly preferable for creating charts.

NOTE   *To create a good chart, your data must be suitable for charting. Numerical data that can be summarized and compared, such as total sales for several months, is a good candidate for charting.*

To send data to Excel for charting:

1. Create a query that contains only the data you'll include in your chart.

2. In the database window, in the Queries group, select the query name.

3. Choose the Tools→Office Links→Analyze It With Microsoft Excel command. The query data appears in an Excel workbook, ready to use as Excel data.

To use the Access Chart Wizard:

1. Create a query that contains only the data you'll include in your chart.

2. In the database window, in the Reports group, click the New button on the database window toolbar.

3. In the New Report dialog box, select the query name in the Choose The Table Or Query Where The Object's Data Comes From box, and then double-click Chart Wizard in the list of wizards.

4. In the first step, double-click the names of the fields you want to include in the chart, then click Next.

5. In the next step, click a chart type, and click Next.

6. In the next step, you can change the layout of the chart series and categories by dragging the field name buttons. To rearrange the field name buttons on the layout, drag the gray name buttons away from the white boxes on the chart layout, and then drag the gray name buttons from the right side of the wizard into the white layout boxes where you want them, (shown in Figure C-4). Click the Preview Chart button in the upper-left corner of the wizard to see what the current layout looks like.

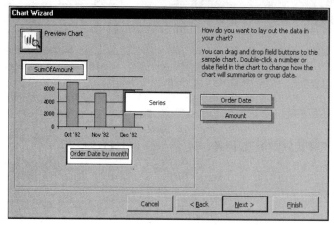

Figure C-4   Laying out the data in a chart.

7. Click Next, type a name for the chart report, and click Finish. The chart will be created as an unreasonably small item on the report page—you need to switch the report to Design view and make the chart bigger.

8. Switch the report to Design view and drag the edges of the report grid down and to the right until the Detail section of the report is big enough to hold a readable chart. Then select the chart and resize it to fill the Detail section. (You'll have to switch back and forth between Print Preview and Design view until you get the chart sized just right.)

Check Box

A check box is a control that displays Yes/No data graphically; a check mark in the check box means Yes (shown in Figure C-5) and a blank check box means No. If a table field has the Yes/No data type assigned, Access will automatically create a check box for the field.

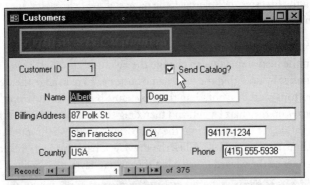

Figure C-5   A marked check box means Yes.

NOTE   *In Access, Yes and No (in a Yes/No data type field) are actually numeric values, and can be calculated. Yes is equal to the value -1, and No is equal to the value 0.*

SEE ALSO *Controls*

Checking Spelling see Spelling

Clipboard

When you work with Microsoft Office applications like Access, the term *clipboard* actually refers to two different items: the system clipboard and the Office clipboard. Both clipboards are temporary storage areas filled with items you cut and copy. However, the two clipboards work differently.

Using the System Clipboard

Whenever you copy or cut something in Windows, Windows stores the copied or cut item on the system clipboard. The system clipboard can store only one item at a time, so when you do copy or cut, the newly copied or cut item replaces the previously copied or cut item.

In non-Microsoft Office Windows programs and when working with Windows itself, you actually copy the contents of the system clipboard to the active window or active workbook when you paste an item.

The system clipboard gets erased in two ways: when you turn off your computer and when you specifically tell Office to clear the Office clipboard. When Office clears the Office clipboard, it also clears the system clipboard.

NOTE   *To paste from the system clipboard, you can choose the Edit→Paste command, click the Paste toolbar button, or use the Ctrl+V shortcut.*

Using the Office Clipboard

In Microsoft Office, you can paste from either the system clipboard or the Office clipboard. Unlike the system clipboard, the Office clipboard can store up to twenty-four items. When you copy the twenty-fifth item, Office discards the first, or oldest, item.

To paste from the Office clipboard, first choose the Edit→Office Clipboard command so that the contents of the Office clipboard are listed in the task pane (shown in Figure C-6). Then, click where you want the item pasted, right-click the item you want in the task pane, and choose the Paste command from the shortcut menu.

Figure C-6   The Clipboard task pane.

The Office clipboard lets you copy items between Office documents and programs. For example, you can use the Office clipboard to copy records from an Access table to a Word document or Excel worksheet.

The Office clipboard gets erased when you close the last Office program. You can also erase the Office clipboard by clicking the Clear All button in the Clipboard task pane. (This also clears the system clipboard.) You can erase individual items in the Office clipboard by right-clicking the item and choosing the Delete command.

SEE ALSO *Copying Data and Formulas*

Closing Access

To close, or quit, Access, click the X button in the upper-right corner of the Access window, or choose the File→Exit command.

Closing a Database

To close a database, click the X button in the upper-right corner of the database window, or close all the database objects and then choose the File→Close command.

Closing Database Objects

To close any database object (a form, table, query, report, and so forth), click the X button in the upper-right corner of the object window, or (if the object is the active window) choose the File→Close command.

Forms will often have a command button that's labeled Close, especially if there's no X button in the upper-right corner. When you create a form, you can disable the X button and create a command button to close the form instead.

SEE ALSO *Forms*

Coloring

You can add color or change the color of most parts of Access forms and reports, but not tables and queries. To color controls or backgrounds, switch the form or report to Design view.

Coloring Text

To color the text in a specific control or label, select the control or label. Then click the Font/Fore Color toolbar button's arrow to display a palette of colors. Click the color you want for the selected control.

NOTE   *You cannot color individual characters in a control—the control's entire text is colored one color.*

Coloring a Form Background

To fill a form background with a color, switch to Design view. Right-click the form grid and click Properties. On the Format tab, click in the Back Color box, click the Build button that appears (the button with three dots), and click the color you want (shown in Figure C-7). Each section of a form (Header, Detail, and Footer) has its own background color set separately, so if your form has more than one section, set the color for each section.

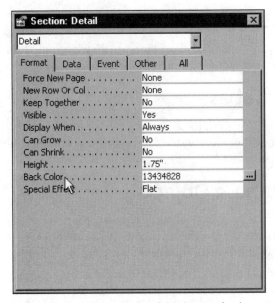

Figure C-7   Setting a form's background color.

Coloring Controls

To color a control or some part of a control, click the control (or part of the control) that you want to color. Use the various buttons on the Formatting toolbar to color, set line thickness, and add special effects to controls (shown in Figure C-8).

Figure C-8   The buttons for formatting controls.

Columns see Field

Combo Box

A combo box (shown in Figure C-9) is a control that allows you to select a value from a list or type a new value into the list. It's used by a lookup field to look up values in another table or in a list you create.

Figure C-9   A combo box control in a form.

SEE ALSO *Controls*

Command Button

A command button (shown in Figure C-10) is a button-shaped control in a form that runs a macro or carries out an event procedure. You can use the Control Wizard to create a command button that works with VBA programming code (which the wizard writes for you), or you can create your own command button that runs one of your macros when it's clicked.

Figure C-10 Command button controls in a form.

SEE ALSO *Controls*

Comparison Operators see Criteria Operators

Concatenate

To concatenate values is to join two values so they are displayed as a single value. For example, if you concatenate a FirstName field to a LastName field, as in the expression **[FirstName]&[LastName]**, the two names are displayed as a full name in a single field (although in this expression, there's no space between the two names). To create a space between the names, you need to concatenate a space character into the expression, like this: [FirstName]&" "&[LastName].

Conditional Formatting

Conditional formatting is control formatting that changes according to the value that's displayed in the control. For example, a report can have a text box control with text that's formatted bold whenever the value in the control is greater than $100. Conditional formatting can be applied to controls in forms and reports.

Setting Conditional Formatting in Forms and Reports

To conditionally format a control, open the form or report in Design view and select the control. Choose the Format→Conditional Formatting command.

17

In the Conditional Formatting dialog box (shown in Figure C-11), set a condition starting in the leftmost box under Condition 1. Set the conditions by choosing an operator in the second box, and entering criteria in the remaining box(es). Then use the formatting buttons to set the formatting for the control whenever the displayed value meets the conditions.

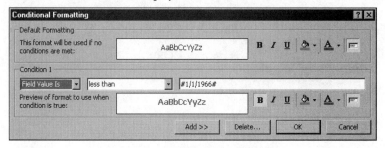

Figure C-11   The Conditional Formatting dialog box, set to format birthdays prior to 1966 in bold and red.

To set another condition for the same control, click the Add button and create the next set of conditional formatting. You can set up to three conditional formats for a single control.

Deleting Conditional Formatting

To delete a conditional format, open the form or report in Design view, select the control, and choose the Format→Conditional Formatting command.

Click the Delete button, and in the Delete Conditional Format dialog box, (shown in Figure C-12), mark the check box for each condition you want to delete.

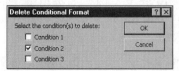

Figure C-12   Deleting conditional formatting.

Control Box

The control box is the icon in the upper-left corner of each window—it displays the control menu when clicked. You can hide it (along with the Min/Max/Close buttons) in forms you create by choosing No in the Control Box property on the Format tab in the Form properties sheet.

Controls

A control is an object on a form or report that displays data, performs an action, or adds graphics to the form or report. Some examples are text boxes, labels, image controls, option buttons, command buttons, and subform controls.

Bound and Unbound Controls

A *bound* control is a control that displays the data in a specific field in a table or query—the control is bound to that field. An *unbound* control is one that doesn't display data from a table or query field. Examples of unbound controls are labels that display helpful messages for users, and pictures (such as company logos) that don't change as the data changes. Here are some more things to know about bound controls:

- Bound controls can be used to enter data in a form—unbound controls cannot be used to enter data.

- Bound controls have labels attached that show the field name. You can change the text in the label, but don't change the field name in the control.

- A bound control's label can be moved separately from the control, if you drag the label by the small box in its upper-left corner (when you point your mouse at that box, the mouse icon looks like a hand with one finger pointing).

- You can also delete a control's label—click the label and press Delete—but if you delete the control itself, the label is also deleted.

Creating Controls on Forms

To add a control to a form, open the form in Design view. If the Toolbox and the field list are not displayed, click the Toolbox and Field List buttons on the Form Design toolbar to display them (shown in Figure C-13).

Figure C-13   A field list and the Toolbox.

19

To create an unbound control, click the button for the control in the Toolbox, then click in the form grid where you want to place the control (you'll probably need to move the control around after it's in place).

To create a bound control, click the button for the control in the Toolbox, then drag the bound field from the Field List and drop it in the form grid.

Some controls are most easily created using the Control Wizard, which is a button in the upper-right corner of the Toolbox. If the Control Wizard button is turned on, it's highlighted (as shown in Figure C-14), and when you click a control button and then drag a field from the field list to the form or report, the wizard for that control will start.

Figure C-14 When the Control Wizard button (in the upper-right corner of the Toolbox) is highlighted, the wizard starts when you create a control that requires it.

Label Control

Label controls aren't bound to fields, and you can use them to make forms more efficient. For example, you can place an unbound label at the top of a group of controls to identify them (as shown in Figure C-15), rather than labeling each individual control separately. And you can create them to remind users of procedures and shortcuts.

Figure C-15 An unbound label that identifies a group of controls.

To create a label, click the Label button in the Toolbox, and then click in the form or report where you want to place the label. Type your label text—as you type, the label expands to fit your text. Click away from the label when you finish.

You can also click the Label button in the Toolbox, and then drag to draw a label of the size you want before you type the label text. The label remains the size you drew until you resize it.

Text Box

A text box can be bound to a field in the underlying table or query (shown in Figure C-16), or be unbound and used as a calculated control. To create a text box, click the Text Box button in the Toolbox, then click in the form or report (for an unbound text box) or drag the bound field from the field list and drop it in the form or report (for a bound text box).

GiftpakName	FruitName	Quantity
10-Star Any Occasion Treasure		
	Apple	4
	Apricot	6
	Kiwi	6
	Peach	2
	Plum	6
	Prune	12
5-Star Any Occasion Treasure		
	Apricot	4
	Cherry, Bing	12
	Orange	3
	Peach	3

Figure C-16   All the information in this report is contained in bound text boxes.

Check Box, Toggle Button, Option Button

All of these controls (shown in Figure C-17) do the same thing—they record Yes or No entries in a table field. They are best suited to fields with a Yes/No data type, and they don't use a Control Wizard. To create a bound check box, toggle button, or option button, click the control's button in the Toolbox, then drag the bound field from the field list to the form.

Figure C-17   A check box, toggle button, and option button on a form.

Option Group

The option group control, shown in Figure C-18, gives a user a choice of predetermined entries for a field (which makes your database a bit more bulletproof because incorrect entries cannot be made in the field). You use a wizard to set up the option group control, and the option group should have an option button in it for each possible entry in the field. To create an option group, be sure the Control Wizard button in the Toolbox is highlighted, click the Option Group button in the Toolbox, and then click in the form grid.

Next, follow the wizard steps: enter the label names for each button you want in the option group, choose a default button that will be chosen for new entries, set the values that will be entered in the field by each button in the group, and select the field where the control's values will be entered. When you get to the fourth wizard step, you have the options to Save The Value For Later Use or Store The Value In This Field. Choose the Store The Value In This Field option and select the table field where the value should be entered. Then choose a visual design and give the control an identifiable name.

Figure C-18   An option group control for bulletproof data entry in a form.

NOTE   *Enclosing multiple option buttons or check boxes in a rectangle is not the same as creating an option group control.*

Combo Box, List Box

The combo box and list box (shown in Figure C-19) are identical, except that the combo box takes less space on a form because when it's not in use, it's "rolled up" to the size of a text box.

Figure C-19 A combo box and list box for data entry on a form.

The combo box and list box use a wizard. To create either control, make sure the Control Wizard button in the Toolbox is highlighted, then click the control button and click in the form grid.

Next, follow the wizard steps: in the first step, shown in Figure C-20, you can choose to have the control look up values that are in another table or query, or you can create a static lookup list by choosing the I Will Type In The Values That I Want option. (The option you choose in the first step determines the next wizard steps you see.)

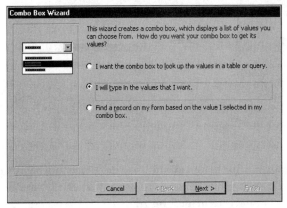

Figure C-20 Choose how the combo box or list box will get its values.

If you chose the I Want The Combo Box To Look Up The Values In A Table Or Query option, the next three steps will guide you through choosing the table/query and the field where the data entries will be looked up. If you chose the I Will Type In The Values That I Want option, the next wizard step asks you to type in the allowable entries for the field.

The next wizard step lets you select the field where the control's values will be entered, and the last step asks you to give the control an identifiable name.

Command Button

Command buttons are designed to trigger an action when they're clicked. They're often used to close forms, open other forms, or print reports, and they make it very easy for an inexperienced user to work in a database.

You can let the Control Wizard create a command button for you that performs a common action using a VBA (Visual Basic for Applications) procedure, or you can create your own macro to run a procedure and then attach the macro to a command button.

To create a command button using the wizard: make sure the Control Wizard button in the Toolbox is highlighted, then click the Command Button button and click in the form grid. The wizard starts, and you choose a category of actions, and then a specific action for the command button to perform (shown in Figure C-21). Follow the wizard steps to choose an image or text for the command button's label and a name for the button.

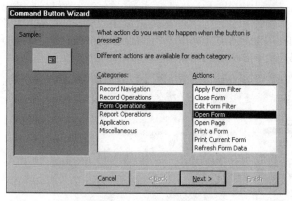

Figure C-21 Choose a VBA action for a wizard-created command button.

To create a command button to which you can attach your own macro: turn the Control Wizard button in the Toolbox off, then click the Command Button button and click in the form grid.

Create the macro that the button will run, then right-click the new command button and click Properties. On the Event tab, click in the On Click property box, and click the arrow that appears on the right of the box. Select the macro you want to attach from the list.

To change the label on a command button: Click the label to select it, then select and delete the existing text and type a new label.

Image, Unbound Object Frame, Bound Object Frame

Image controls, unbound object frames, and bound object frames all hold pictures on forms and reports.

A bound object frame holds pictures (and other OLE objects, such as graphs, sound files, and video) that are entered in a table field. This control is appropriate for displaying, for example, pictures of employees in an employee information form, or pictures of products in a catalog-style report.

An unbound object frame holds embedded OLE objects (such as pictures, graphs, sound files, and video) that are not entered in a table and don't change when the displayed record changes.

An image control is used to display pictures that are not entered in a table and don't change when the displayed record changes—it uses fewer database resources than an unbound object frame, and if you need to display a picture, such as a logo on a form or report, an image control is preferable to an unbound object frame.

To create an image control: click the Image button in the Toolbox, then click in the form or report grid. An Insert Picture dialog box opens, shown in Figure C-22. Navigate to the picture you want and double-click the picture file name. You can move and resize the picture after it's inserted.

Figure C-22   The Insert Picture dialog box.

To create a bound object frame: Display the field list and Toolbox. Click the Bound Object Frame button in the Toolbox, then drag the object's field from the field list and drop it in the form or report grid.

To create an unbound object frame: Click the Unbound Object Frame button in the Toolbox, then click in the form or report grid. A Microsoft Access dialog box opens (shown in Figure C-23).

C

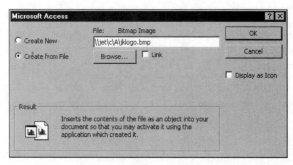

Figure C-23   The dialog box for inserting an object in an unbound object frame.

If the object already exists, click the Create From File option, click the Browse button to navigate to the object file, double-click the file name, and click OK to insert it.

If the object hasn't been created yet, click the Create New option, select a program in the Object Type list, and click OK. A small window in your form or report grid appears, and the tools for the program you selected appear. Create the new object in the small program window that opens. When you finish creating the object, click away from the control in the form or report grid. To edit the object later: double-click the unbound object frame, make changes using the object's program tools that appear, and click away from the object when you finish.

Page Break

Page break controls can be used to create multiple pages in a form and page breaks in a report.

A page break in a form breaks a large form into multiple pages. When entering data, you move from one page to another by pressing the Page Up and Page Down keys. A page break in a report forces the printed report pages to start a new page.

To use a page break in a form or report, click the Page Break button in the Toolbox, and then click in the form or report grid on the left margin.

NOTE   *Page breaks are not the best way to break large pages in either a form or a report. Reports are best broken into pages with their report properties, and large forms are easier to use if they're broken into pages with tab controls.*

SEE ALSO   *Reports*

Tab Control

A tab control in a form allows you to display a form in a multiple-page format, with tabbed page selectors along the top of the form (as shown in Figure C-24).

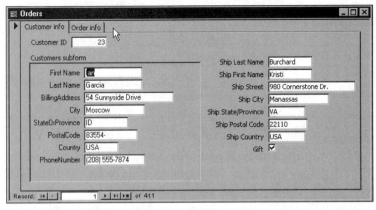

Figure C-24   A large form is more efficient with multiple, tabbed pages.

When you create tabbed pages in a form, you add tab controls to the form, and then move the controls to the tabbed pages. The tabbed pages sit on the form background, underneath the data controls. To create a multi-page tabbed form:

1. Open a form in Design view. You can start with a wizard-created form (because the connection to the underlying table or query is already made), and either delete all the existing controls and re-create them later or cut-and-paste the existing controls on top of the new tab controls.

2. In the Toolbox, click the Tab Control button, then click in the form's background. A tab control with two tabs appears in the form (as shown in Figure C-25). Resize the tab controls, if you need to, to make them fit the form grid.

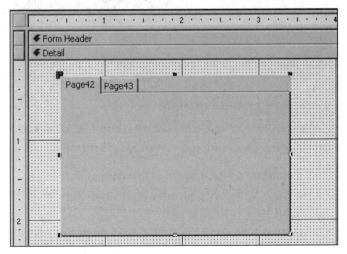

Figure C-25   A new tab control in a form's Design view.

TIP   *To select the entire tab control (to move, resize, or delete it), click in the area at the top of the control, to the right of the tabs. To select an individual tab page (to create or paste controls on the page), click the tab for that page.*

3. Create new controls on a specific tab page, or cut existing controls and then paste them on the specific tab page.

   • To cut a control, select it and press Ctrl+X; to paste the cut control, click the tab for the page you want, and then press Ctrl+V.

   • To create a new control on the tabbed page, click the tab for the page you want, then click the control in the Toolbox, drag the field name from the field list, and drop it on the tab control.

TIP   *If you need more room to work, maximize the form window.*

4. To change a tab caption, double-click the tab. In the Page properties sheet, on the Format tab, type a tab name in the Caption property box.

5. Resize the tab control as needed to fit the controls, and then resize the form grid to fit the tab control (shown in Figure C-26).

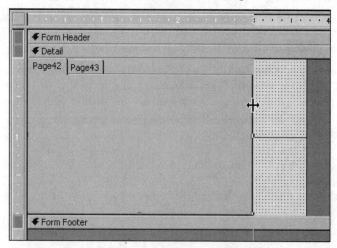

Figure C-26   Drag the form grid border to fit the tab control.

Here are a few ways to change the tabbed pages:

   • To add another tabbed page to the tab control, right-click in the tab control and click Insert Page.

   • To delete a tabbed page, right-click the tab for the page and click Delete Page.

- To rearrange the page order (the order in which the tabs appear from left to right), right-click the tab control and click Page Order, then use the Move Up and Move Down buttons in the Page Order dialog box to rearrange the page tabs.

Rectangle, Line

Rectangles and lines are graphical objects you draw and format on forms and reports to make the data and controls easier to read and use. To draw a rectangle or line, click the button in the Toolbox and then drag to draw the object in the form or report grid. To format rectangles and lines with different colors and line widths, select the object(s) and use the buttons on the Formatting toolbar.

Subform/Subreport

A subform is a small form window in a larger form, which shows records from a different table or query that are related to the record shown in the larger, or *main*, form window. Figure C-27 shows an Orders main form with an Items subform—the Items subform shows the items that are included in the order that's in the main form. The subform is contained in a Subform/Subreport control.

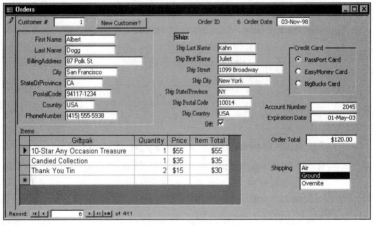

Figure C-27 Subform records are related to the main form record.

You can create a subform in a main form in several ways:

- By using the Form Wizard and building a form from two related tables (the wizard creates the main form and subform for you).

- By creating a separate form for the subform, and then dragging the subform name from the database window onto the main form in Design view.

- By opening the main form in Design view, and using a Subform/Subreport control to create the subform.

To use the Subform/Subreport control to build a subform in a main form:

1. Make sure the Control Wizard button is highlighted in the Toolbox. Click the Subform/Subreport button in the Toolbox, and click in the main form grid.

2. In the Subform Wizard, choose whether you're creating the subform from a table or query or from a form you've already created.

3. Choose the fields that link the subform to the main form, and give the subform control a name.

SEE ALSO *Forms*

Creating Controls on Reports

You create controls on reports in the same way that you create them on forms. The biggest differences are that not all controls are suitable to reports (because reports don't take data entry), and controls behave differently in the different sections of a report.

In general, when a control is placed in a report's Detail section, the control displays the detail data for every record in the underlying table or query. If you want to display summary data for a group of records, instead of each detail, it's easiest to use the Report Wizard to create a grouped report for you.

TIP   *A good way to create a printed form that people can fill out with pencils is to use unbound controls, such as text boxes, check boxes, and option buttons, on a report.*

Setting Default Control Types

If you find that you are consistently changing the properties of a particular control (for example, the label font for command buttons), you can save yourself the constant changes by changing the default properties of a control.

To change the default properties of a control: click the control's button in the Toolbox, then click the Properties button on the Design toolbar. Change the properties that you always change. The default properties for that control will remain changed for that form or report until you change them again (but the properties won't be changed for other forms and reports).

Copying and Pasting Duplicate Controls

Copying and pasting duplicate controls is a much more efficient way to create a set of identical controls on a form or report.

To copy and paste identical controls, as shown in Figure C-28, make sure there's room for the pasted controls beneath the control you're going to copy. Then select the control you want to copy, press Ctrl+C, and then press Ctrl+V repeatedly until you've made all the copies you need. (Don't click anything in between pressing Ctrl+C to copy and pressing Ctrl+V to paste.) All the new copies will be pasted in a column below the original control.

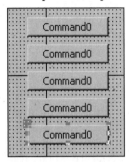

Figure C-28   Identical controls are easy when you copy and paste them.

If you copy a control and then click elsewhere in the form or report grid before pasting, the new copy will be pasted in the upper-left corner of the grid and you can move it to wherever you need it.

TIP   *You can also use the Edit→Copy and Edit→Paste commands, but you may find Ctrl+C and Ctrl+V are easier once you begin using them.*

Moving Controls

When you create a form or report, you'll want to move controls to make them fit the page better, or to create a more visually pleasing arrangement.

To move a control, select the control, then hover your mouse over the control until the mouse pointer becomes an open-hand symbol (shown in Figure C-29). Press the mouse button and drag the control where you need it.

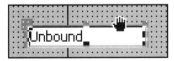

Figure C-29   The "move" pointer.

Bound controls have labels that move with them—whether you move the control or the label, they move together. If you need to move either the control or the label separately, point to the box in the upper-left corner of the item you want to move, and when the mouse pointer is a hand with one finger pointing up, press the mouse button and drag the item where you need it.

If you have multiple controls all neatly arranged and you need to move the whole group, you can select the entire group and then move it with the "move" pointer (the open-hand symbol), as shown in Figure C-30.

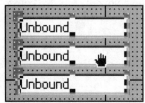

Figure C-30   Moving a selected group of controls.

Sizing Controls

To size a control manually, select the control. Drag one of the handles around the control's perimeter to resize it to the size and shape you want. You can also have Access do the resizing for you, like this:

- To resize a label to fit its text, select the label, then choose the Format→Size→To Fit command. You can also select several labels, and resize them all to fit their own text with this one command.

- To resize several controls to match the tallest, shortest, widest, or narrowest among the group, select all the controls, and then choose the Format→Size command that fits your purpose. If, for example, you choose the Format→Size→To Widest command, all the selected controls will be resized to the width of the widest selected control.

Disabling Controls

Sometimes you need to display data in a form, but you don't want anyone to edit that displayed data (for example, an ID number). You can prevent edits to displayed data by disabling and locking a control. *Disabling* a control prevents it from being selected when a user presses the Tab key or click the control. *Locking* a control prevents a user from entering or editing data in the control. Used together, disabling and locking are an effective way to display data for a record without allowing any changes to the data.

- To disable a control, open the form in Design view, right-click the control, and click Properties. On the Data tab, click in the Enabled property box and select No.

- To lock a control, open the form in Design view, right-click the control, and click Properties. On the Data tab, click in the Locked property box, and select Yes.

Selecting Multiple Controls

Some procedures, such as sizing and moving, need to be performed on a group of controls together. To select a group of controls, do one of these two things:

- Select the first control, then hold down the Shift key while you click the remaining controls to select them.

- If the controls are adjacent to each other, use your mouse to draw a "lasso" that touches or surrounds each control you want to select, as shown in Figure C-31.

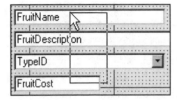

Figure C-31 "Lassoing" several controls.

Aligning Controls

Aligning controls manually is very difficult, but if you let Access do the aligning for you, precisely aligned controls are easy. Here are some techniques for aligning controls:

- Choose the Format→Snap To Grid command to turn on grid-snapping. When you move a control, it "snaps" to the nearest gridline in the form or report grid.

- Select a control, then hold down the Ctrl key while you use the arrow keys on your keyboard to "nudge" the control in very small increments.

- Select a group of controls, choose the Format→Align commands to align the controls in the group with one another. If, for example, you choose the Format→Align→Left command, all the selected controls will be aligned with the left edge of the leftmost-selected control.

Converting Older Databases see Versions, Converting

Copying Controls

To copy the selected controls, choose the Edit→Copy command (or press Ctrl+C), click in the form or report grid, and then choose the Edit→Paste command (or press Ctrl+V). The new copy is pasted in the upper-left corner of the form or report section you clicked in.

SEE ALSO *Controls*

Copying Data and Formulas

To copy data in a table or form, you can use any of these techniques:

• Select the characters in a cell or text box, then press Ctrl+C or choose the Edit→Copy command. The data is copied to the clipboard, and you can paste it in another cell or text box, another table in the database, another database, or another file such as an Excel worksheet.

• Select one or more records in a table or query, then press Ctrl+C or choose the Edit→Copy command. The records are copied to the clipboard, and you can paste them in another table in the database, another database, or another file such as an Excel worksheet.

• In a table, to copy the data from the cell directly above, click in the cell where you want to paste the copied data, and press Ctrl+".

Copying Database Objects

To copy a form, report, or query, display the group (Forms, Reports, or Queries) in the database window. Right-click the name of the object you want to copy, and click Copy. Then right-click in a blank area of the database window and click Paste. Type a name for the new object in the Paste As dialog box.

To copy a table, display the Tables group in the database window. Right-click the name of the table you want to copy, and click Copy. Then right-click in a blank area of the database window and click Paste. Type a name for the new table in the Paste Table As dialog box, and choose an option—Structure Only creates a copy of the table with no data, Structure And Data creates a copy of the table with all data included, and Append Data To Existing Table is for copying the data from one table into another table.

NOTE   *If you choose the Append Data To Existing Table option, don't type a new table name—instead, in the Table Name box, type the name of the table to which you want to append the copied data.*

TIP   *If you're about to make structural changes to a database object,
            make a copy of the object and make the changes in the copy. If
            the changes go well, delete the original object, save the new object
            with the original name, and re-create any relationships. If the
            changes don't go well and the object breaks, you can delete it
            and start again, because you haven't broken the original.*

Copying Databases

To copy a database file, open the My Computer window to the folder where
your existing database is saved. Right-click the name of the database file,
and click Copy. Then right-click in a blank area of the folder window and click
Paste. A copy of the database file is pasted, with the name **Copy of** *filename*
(shown in Figure C-32). Right-click the new file name and click Rename,
then type a name for the new database file.

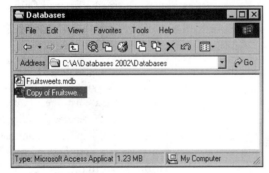

Figure C-32   A copied database file in a folder window.

Copying Formatting

To copy formatting, select the control you want to copy, click the Format
Painter button on the Formatting toolbar, and click the control to which you
want to copy the formatting. To copy formatting to several other controls,
double-click the Format Painter button, and click each control to which you
want to copy the formatting. When you're done, click the Format Painter
button again to turn it off.

Criteria

Criteria are limiting conditions, such as "Arizona" or ">100", used in queries and filters to show a limited set of records.

Criteria Operators

Here are some common criteria operators for filters and queries, and examples from a database of fruit products:

OPERATOR	PURPOSE	EXAMPLES
And	Records having one characteristic AND another characteristic	**like *fr* and like *cal*** (records that contain the words "Fresh" and "California" in the filtered field)
Or	Records having one characteristic OR another characteristic	**apple or kiwi** (records that contain the word "Apple" or the word "Kiwi" in the filtered field)
Not	Records that do not have a specified characteristic	**not apple** (any value other than Apple)
&	Concatenates fields into a single column	**[City]&", "&[State]&" "&[Zip]** (in a Customers table, concatenates the City, State, and Zip fields, commas, and spaces into an address line such as "Rathdrum, ID 83858")
Like	Records having the criteria as part of a field's value	**like a*** (entries that start with the letter A); **like *son** (entries that end with "son"); **like [t-v]*** (entries that start with the letters T, U, or V); **like *ba*** (entries that include the letter sequence "ba")
Between... And	Records having a value between two values you specify	**between 1/1/98 and 2/1/98** (values from January 2, 1998, through January 31, 1998)
In	Records with a characteristic in a list you supply	**in(Dried,Candied)** (a value of Dried or Candied; same result as **Dried OR Candied**)

OPERATOR	PURPOSE	EXAMPLES
Is Null	Records having no entry in the field	**is null** (in a PhoneNumber field finds records with no phone number entered)
Is Not Null	Records having an entry in the field	**is not null** (in a PhoneNumber field finds records with a phone number entered)
=, <>, >, <	Indicates equal, unequal, greater than, less than	**=42** (entries of 42); **<>3** (entries other than 3); **>1/1/98** (dates after January 1, 1998); **<10.50** (values less than 10.50)
*, /, +, -	Multiplies, divides, adds, subtracts	**[Price]*[Quantity]** (multiply the value in the Price field by the value in the Quantity field); **[Weight]/12** (divide the value in the Weight field by 12)

Crosstab Query

A crosstab query is a query that displays values in a spreadsheet-style table, with one field's entries listed as row headings and another field's entries listed as column headings, and a numeric field summarized in the intersections. The example in Figure C-33 shows a crosstab query of fruit packages, called Giftpaks, and the numbers of each kind of fruit contained in each giftpak.

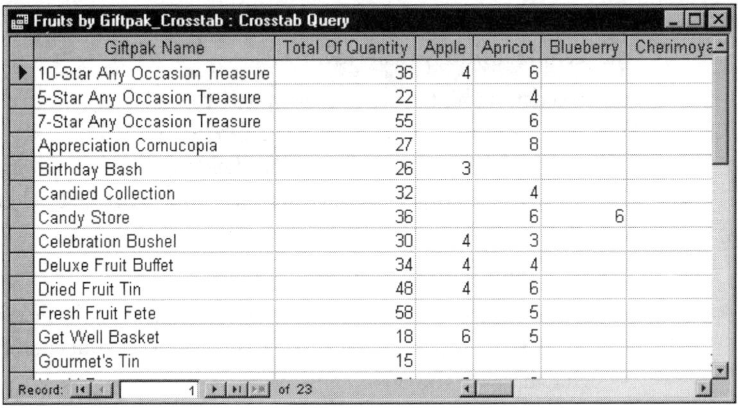

Fruits by Giftpak_Crosstab : Crosstab Query

Giftpak Name	Total Of Quantity	Apple	Apricot	Blueberry	Cherimoya
10-Star Any Occasion Treasure	36	4	6		
5-Star Any Occasion Treasure	22		4		
7-Star Any Occasion Treasure	55		6		
Appreciation Cornucopia	27		8		
Birthday Bash	26	3			
Candied Collection	32		4		
Candy Store	36		6	6	
Celebration Bushel	30	4	3		
Deluxe Fruit Buffet	34	4	4		
Dried Fruit Tin	48	4	6		
Fresh Fruit Fete	58		5		
Get Well Basket	18	6	5		
Gourmet's Tin	15				

Record: 1 of 23

Figure C-33 A crosstab query.

SEE ALSO *Queries*

Ctrl (^) Symbol see AutoKeys

Currency Symbols

The currency symbols Access can apply to a number's display format depend on the regional settings selected for Windows. You can choose the currency symbol from among those available when you choose the display format for a field or control.

SEE ALSO *Field Properties, Formatting Data*

Customizing Toolbars see Toolbars

Cutting

If you need to move data, rather than copy it, you can select the data and use the Cut toolbar button or the Edit→Cut command to remove the selected data, and then paste the cut item wherever you want.

Data

Data is the information stored in a table in a database. Data can be names, dates, telephone numbers, number values, yes or no, long text notes, or anything else that you need to record.

Entering Data

You can enter data directly into the table's datasheet, or you can enter data through a form. Whether you enter data directly into a table or using a form, the techniques are virtually identical.

To enter data, move the insertion point into the field where you want to make an entry, type the entry, and press the Tab key or the Enter key to move to the next field. When you reach the last field in the record, pressing the Tab key or the Enter key moves the insertion point to the first field in the next record.

Here are some more data entry techniques:

- If you enter data in a lookup field, you can either click the field's arrow and select an entry or type the first one or two letters of your entry (the lookup field will select the correct entry).
- You can enter the current date by pressing Ctrl+: (colon).

- You can copy a field's entry from the preceding record (the record immediately above) by pressing Ctrl+' (apostrophe).

- In a form, you can move to the same field in the next record or the preceding record by pressing the Page Up and Page Down keys.

- In a table, you can move to the same field in the next record or the preceding record by pressing the up and down arrow keys.

- In a form with a subform, pressing the Tab key will move the insertion point into the subform, but the insertion point will remain in the subform until you move back to the main form by clicking in a control in the main form.

- You can also just click in the field where you want to enter data.

Editing Data

Data can be edited directly in the table, in a form, and often in a query, using the same editing techniques. To edit data, drag to select the characters you want to remove or replace (as shown in Figure D-1), and then type the new characters or press Delete to remove the selected characters.

Figure D-1   Selecting characters to edit.

Calculating Data

Data can be calculated in a query (in a calculated field) and in forms and reports (in calculated controls). All data calculations are performed by expressions, which use any combination of mathematical operators, field names enclosed in square brackets, and formula functions.

Figure D-2 shows an example of a calculated field in a query. In the expression entered in the Field row, the characters left of the colon are the caption for the field in Datasheet view, and the expression right of the colon consists of the field name (Price) enclosed in square brackets, a multiplication symbol (*), and the number (1.1) by which each value in the Price field is multiplied.

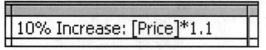

Figure D-2   A calculated field in a query.

Figure D-3 shows an example of a calculated control in a report. This calculated control is in a report's Group Footer section, and it uses a SUM function to sum the values in the Amount field for each group. The function's arguments (in this case, just the Amount field) are enclosed in parentheses, and the field name (Amount) is enclosed in square brackets.

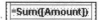

Figure D-3   A calculated control in a report.

SEE ALSO   *Expression, Functions, Lookup Fields, Subform Control, Subforms*

Data Access Pages

A data access page is an interactive web page that's linked to your database, and works like a database form; it can be opened in a web browser and used to enter and edit data in a database without opening the actual database.

Creating Data Access Pages with the Wizard

To create a data access page from an existing database object, select the name of the object in the database window, and then select Page from the New Object button on the Access toolbar.

NOTE   *You can create data access pages from forms and reports, but the Page Wizard works more efficiently from tables and queries.*

In the New Data Access Page dialog box, be sure the name of the selected object appears in the Choose The Table Or Query box, and then double-click Page Wizard. In the first Wizard step, double-click each field you want to include in your page; choose a grouping field (if you want one); choose a sort order; and give the page a name.

The new page opens in Design view (shown in Figure D-4), but the page is functional and doesn't need any changes.

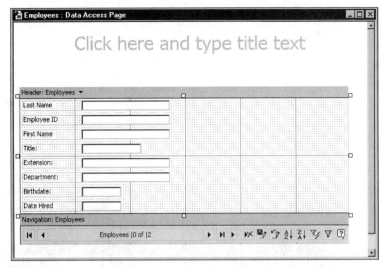

Figure D-4   A new data access page in Design view.

To save and close the new page, choose the File→Close command. When you are asked if you want to save changes to the design of the new page, click Yes. In the Save As Data Access Page dialog box, navigate to the folder where you want to save the page file (if other people need to open your new page, save the page in a folder they have access to). Give the new page a name in the File Name box and click Save. A link to the page file is saved in the Pages group in the database window.

Modifying Data Access Pages

To modify or edit a data access page, open the Pages group in the database window, click the page name, and click the Design button on the database window toolbar.

In Design view, you can reposition and resize controls, format text and colors, and add and remove fields in the same way as in a form's Design view.

Using Data Access Pages in a Web Browser

To open a data access page in a web browser, the Office XP Active Web Components must be installed in the machine where the browser is installed. If your data access page is opened in the computer in which you created it, the data access page will open in your browser because your computer has the Office XP Active Web Components installed. If, however, you attempt to open the data access page in a computer that doesn't have the Office XP

Active Web components installed, you won't be able to open the page unless you download and install the Office XP Active Web components.

When you create a data access page, the data access page file is stored in the hard drive or network folder where you saved it. A link, or shortcut, to the page is created in the Pages group in your database window. Anyone can open your data access page (if they have the Office XP Active Web components installed) by navigating to the folder and double-clicking your data access page.

The data access page opens into a browser window, and looks like the one shown in Figure D-5. It works just like an Access form. The buttons on the toolbar at the bottom of the page all have ScreenTips to identify them. The data displayed in a data access page can be sorted, filtered, edited, saved, and deleted using the toolbar buttons.

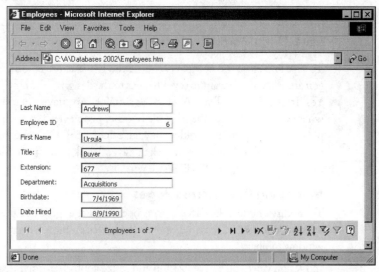

Figure D-5   A data access page in a browser window.

NOTE   *If your data access page doesn't open in your browser after you create it, open your browser window and click File→Work Off-Line to remove the check mark next to the command.*

SEE ALSO *Saving*

Data Types

A data type is a field property that determines what type of data the field can contain (for example: number, text, date/time, or Yes/No). Setting the correct data type for a field is the most basic technique for ensuring data accuracy, because a field won't allow entry of data that doesn't meet the data type.

Data type is assigned to fields in a table's Design view, by selecting the data type from a list in the Data Type column, as shown in Figure D-6.

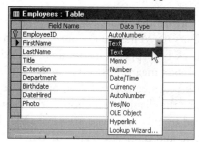

Figure D-6   Assigning a data type to a field.

Here's a list of the data types for Access fields:

DATA TYPE	DESCRIPTION
Text	For entries that aren't meant to be calculated, such as names, street addresses, Social Security numbers, and telephone numbers. A text field entry cannot be longer than 255 characters.
Memo	For long entries, such as notes about an employee or long, detailed descriptions of a product.
Number	For numbers that can be calculated, such as quantities. For money, use the Currency data type instead.
Date/Time	For dates and times.
Currency	For currency values such as price or cost.

DATA TYPE	DESCRIPTION
AutoNumber	For automatic entry of non-repeating, sequential numbers that uniquely identify a record in a table. An AutoNumber entry is never repeated in the table; even if records are deleted, the AutoNumber entry assigned to that record won't be reassigned to a new record. This data type is most appropriate for a primary key field.
Yes/No	For entries that must be Yes/No, True/False, or On/Off. When you choose this data type, a check box appears in the field. Marking the check box means Yes, True, or On; an empty check box means No, False, or Off. Regardless of the display you choose, the values stored by this data type are -1 for Yes, True, or On, and 0 for No, False, or Off.
OLE Object	For storing text, spreadsheets, pictures, sounds, and other data created in Word, Excel, or other programs. If, for example, you want to enter employee pictures in an Employees table, use the OLE Object data type.
Hyperlink	For entries that are hyperlinks to Internet, intranet, hard drive, or network locations. Clicking a hyperlink entry opens the document that the hyperlink points to, and can be very useful in a form.
Lookup Wizard	For choosing entries from either another table or from a list of entries you create. When you choose this data type, the Lookup Wizard helps you create the lookup list you want for the field.

NOTE   *To stop problems before they start, assign a Number data type only to fields in which the number values will be calculated. If a field's data appears to be numbers, but won't be calculated, assign the Text data type (the data will sort and filter better).*

TIP   *Be consistent in the data types you assign, so that you won't be spending lots of time checking data types before joining tables.*

Data Types, Matching

When two tables are related, the specific fields that are joined must have matching data types.

Matching usually means the *same*, but not always. When one of the related fields has a data type of AutoNumber, the matching data type in the related field is Number, with a Size property of Long Integer.

SEE ALSO *Junction Table, Relationships*

Data Validation

You can protect data accuracy by creating validation rules, which don't allow any entries that don't meet the rules you set for the field, and validation text, which informs the user of the problem when an invalid entry is made.

SEE ALSO *Validation Rules, Validation Text*

Database

A database collects information, or data, related to a particular topic or entity such as a business or an event. It's a single file that contains tables of all the data pertaining to that entity. Databases usually also contain queries (to filter and display a specific portion of data), forms (to make data entry easier), and reports (to summarize and print specific data in an easy-to-read format), all of which make the collection of information more usable.

Database, Creating

There are two ways to create a database in Access. You can use the Database Wizard to help you create a somewhat-customized pre-built database, or you can build the database yourself.

Creating a Database Using the Wizard

If you want a database that you can use right away, and there's a wizard-built database that meets your needs, the Database Wizard is a good way to go.

NOTE   *When the wizard builds a database, the wizard uses VBA programming to create some of the automation and functionality in the database. The resulting database may be more difficult for you to modify and further customize.*

To create a new database using the Database Wizard:

1. In the New File task pane, under New From Template, click General Templates. (If the New File task pane isn't displayed in the Access window, choose the File→New command.)

2. In the Templates dialog box, on the Databases tab (shown in Figure D-7), double-click the icon for the database you want.

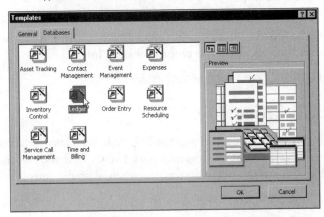

Figure D-7   Double-click a database template to begin creating a new database.

3. In the File New Database dialog box, navigate to the folder where you want to save the database file, type a name for the new database in the File Name box, and click Create. A new database window appears in the Access window, and the Database Wizard starts.

4. Follow the wizard steps to build the database. Each step gives you options for items to include in the new database. You can make the database as simple or as complex as you want, within the limits provided by the wizard. For example, in the second wizard step (shown in Figure D-8), the list on the left shows the available tables in the Asset Tracking database. When you click a table name on the left, the list on the right shows all the available fields for that table. You can include a field by marking its check box, or leave a field out by clearing its check box.

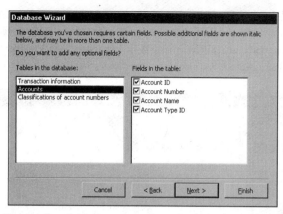

Figure D-8   In the wizard, you choose tables and then choose fields for each table.

5. Continue with the wizard steps to finish the database. After you click Finish, Access builds the new database.

Most wizard-built databases have an opening switchboard. A switchboard is just a database form, but instead of showing a record from a table or query, a switchboard form has buttons that perform actions such as opening other database objects. Switchboards make the database much easier for a non-expert to use, but when you become very comfortable with Access, you'll probably find them a nuisance.

TIP   *If you build a database from scratch and you want a switchboard form, it's easy to build your own.*

Creating a Database Yourself

If you really want to learn about Access, understand how your database works, and want to be able to customize it, you're better off building your new database yourself. (Also, there may not be a wizard-built database that's appropriate for your needs.)

It's not all that difficult to create a database yourself—it's just mysterious at first because it's unlike any other Office program you may have used. Also, it takes more time than using the Database Wizard. To create a database without the wizard:

1. In the New File task pane, under New, click Blank Database. (If the New File task pane isn't displayed in the Access window, choose the File→New command.)

2. In the File New Database dialog box, navigate to the folder where you want to save the database file, type a name for the new database in the File Name box, and click Create. A new database window like the one shown in Figure D-9 appears in your Access window.

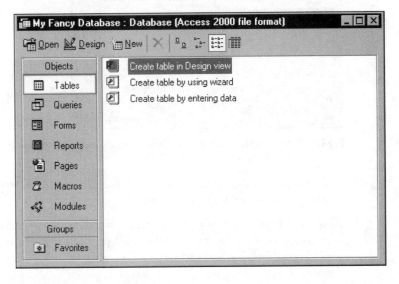

Figure D-9   A new, empty database you create without the wizard.

After you create the database file, you need to create your own database objects. You need to create (or import or link to) tables to store data create and queries, forms, and reports to use the data efficiently.

SEE ALSO *Designing Databases, Forms, Macros, Queries, Report, Tables*

Database Objects

Database objects are the tables, queries, reports, forms, macros, data access pages, and modules that are the functional parts of a database.

To open a specific database object, click the object group name in the Objects bar in the database window shown in Figure D-10, and then double-click the object name.

Figure D-10 The Objects bar is on the left side of the database
window.

To create a new database object, click the object group name in the Objects
bar, and then click the New button in the database window toolbar or click
one of the Create icons in the database window.

Database Window

The database window is the window that appears when you first open a
database. Through the database window you gain access to all the objects
in a database. Database objects (tables, forms, queries, and so forth) are
stored in object groups. You open an object group by clicking the group name
in the Objects bar on the left side of the database window.

SEE ALSO *Windows*

Datasheet View

A Datasheet view (shown in Figure D-11) is a view that displays records
in a row-and-column format similar to a spreadsheet. A Datasheet view
allows you to see many records at the same time.

Supplier ID	Supplier Name	Contact Name	Phone Number
1	WestCoast Fruit and Nut Suppliers	Martin Critton	(415) 555-1221
2	Exotic Fruits, Ltd.	Joanna Paul	(213) 555-8798
3	Growers Cooperative	Terry Miller	(818) 555-1235

Figure D-11 A Datasheet view of a table.

You can show the records in tables, queries, and forms in Datasheet view by clicking the arrow next to the View button on the Access toolbar, and then choosing Datasheet View.

TIP   *If the View button displays an icon of a Datasheet, you don't need to click the arrow—just click the button to switch to Datasheet view.*

SEE ALSO *Views*

Dates

When dates are entered in a table, it's important that the date field be formatted with a Date/Time data type so that Access recognizes the data as dates and can group, calculate, and summarize data based on dates.

NOTE   *If you import data from another program, such as Excel, it's helpful to format the field as a date/time field in Excel before you import data into Access. You're less likely to import invalid entries into the date field, and Access will recognize the entries as dates when you import them.*

SEE ALSO *Formatting Data*

Decimal Values see Field Properties

Deleting

You can delete bits of data, such as an address, from a single record in a table or form, or delete entire records from tables and forms:

- *To delete an item of data* (such as an address) from a specific record, in either a table or a form, drag to select the data item and press Delete.

- *To delete a record from a table,* select the record by clicking the gray record selector box on the left end of the record, and press Delete.

- *To delete a record* from within a form, click in any field in the record, then choose the Edit→Delete Record command. Click Yes when asked if you're sure.

- *To delete an entire field,* or column, of data from a table, open the table in Datasheet view, right-click the field name (the gray column heading), and click Delete Column.

- *To delete a control,* such as a text box, list box, label, or command button, open the form or report in Design view. Click the control you want to delete, and press Delete. (If the control has a bound label which moves with the control, the label is deleted along with the control. To delete the label without deleting its bound control, click the label and press Delete.)

- *To delete a table,* click the object name in the database window, and press Delete. When asked if you're sure, click Yes.

WARNING *Keep in mind that if you delete a table, you won't be able to recover the data directly—you'll have to re-import or re-enter it if you want to get it back.*

- *To delete a database object*—such as a form, report, query, data access page, or macro—click the object name in the database window, and press Delete. (Deleting forms, reports, queries, macros, and data access pages may change the way your database functions, but won't delete data.)

- *To delete a switchboard,* open the Forms group in the database window, click the form named Switchboard, and press Delete.

- *To delete a database* from your hard drive, open a My Computer or Windows Explorer window, and navigate to the folder where your database is stored. Click the database name, and press Delete.

Delimited Text Files

A delimited text file is a text file in which the columns, or fields, of data are separated by a delimiting character such as a comma or a tab character. The delimiting character is recognized by Access when you import a delimited text file into an Access database.

SEE ALSO *Text Files*

Design View

A Design view is a view that allows you to design and change tables, queries, forms, reports, and macros (it's a bit like looking at the object from the back). You can show the records in tables, queries, and forms in Design view by clicking the arrow next to the View button on the Access toolbar, and then choosing Design View. If the view button displays an icon of a triangle-and-pencil, you don't need to click the arrow—just click the button to switch to Design view.

SEE ALSO *Views*

Designing Databases

The key to a functional, efficient database is the design of the database structure and the individual objects in the database. A logical design can save you a lot of time and frustration when you try to make changes to the database later.

Here are some useful guidelines to keep in mind before you begin to create a database:

- Plan your tables and relationships in paper-and-pencil before you begin creating your database—it helps a lot to have a plan to go by.

- Start by thinking about what results and output you want from this database—keep the end result in mind so you can plan for it from the beginning.

- Next, list and organize all the data you have. On paper, organize the data into logical tables that store the data efficiently, and then import or create those tables. Don't worry about adding every field you'll ever need—you can always add new fields to a table later, after the database is finished.

- Separate your data into several fields rather than combining it in a single field. For example, separate names into Title, LastName, FirstName, and MiddleName fields—it's easier to combine these fields when you need to rather than to separate one field into several.

- Keep all the tables for a single event or business in a single database. Don't, for example, have a Customers database and a separate Orders database for the same business entity—that defeats the purpose of using a relational database. Instead, keep the Customers table and the Orders table in one database so you can create a relationship between them.

- Don't keep duplicate sets of data. For example, if you've got a table in Excel that you (or others in your company) need to work with in Excel, you don't need to duplicate the data to use it in Access. Instead, you can link to the Excel table and use its data in Access, thereby keeping just one, current set of data.

- Use limiting Data Types in your fields whenever you can. For example, if a field calls for a Yes or No entry, use a Yes/No data type for that field when you design the table. If the field should look up an entry in another table, use the Lookup Wizard to create a lookup field. The data type can limit the entries to valid entries only, so nobody can enter invalid data.

Detail Section

The Detail section of a report (shown in Figure D-12) is the section where individual records from an underlying table or query are displayed. Any field control placed in the Detail section of a report will display all the individual records in the report's Print Preview (shown in Figure D-14).

Figure D-12   The Detail section in a report's Design view.

Apple	4
Apricot	6
Kiwi	6
Peach	2
Plum	6
Prune	12

Figure D-13   The same Detail section in a report's Print Preview.

SEE ALSO *Report*

Disabling Controls see Controls

Display Format

Display format is the format in which data are displayed in a form or report. The display format may or may not be the same as the value that Access calculates. For example, by changing the Format and Decimal Places properties for a Number field, the value 1.234 can be displayed as 1.23 or 1 or $1.23 or 123%.

SEE ALSO *Formatting Data*

Dynaset

A dynaset is the set of records that results from running a query or a filter (it's also called a recordset).

Editing Data

To edit data, select and replace the characters in the field, or make a different choice in the field's control. Note, however, that you may not be allowed to edit the data if it's in a primary key field, and the table is related to other tables with referential integrity enforced in the join.

SEE ALSO *Referential Integrity*

Editing Records see Records

Erasing Data see Deleting

Error Messages

Error messages appear in calculated fields and calculated controls when there's an error in the expression or formula. In Access, the error messages are not as helpful as in other programs such as Excel. For example, if you create a calculated field in a query that divides a field by zero, you won't see the helpful #DIV/0 message. Instead, you'll see the un-helpful #ERROR message, and you have to figure out what the problem is by yourself.

If you get an #ERROR message in a calculated field or control, here are some things to check:

- Check the mathematical operations. If you get the same error for all the records in your query or report, you might have written a mathematically impossible expression.

- Check the data in the underlying table. If you get the error in just one or a few records, the data may be invalid for the expression you've written. For example, if a table field holds numbers but was given a data type of Text, number values can be entered and calculated. But if an entry contains text characters, that record's field can't be calculated, and you'll see #ERROR.

- If you change a field name in a table while a form or report that references the field is closed, you'll see a #NAME? error in the control for that field next time you open the forms or report. To fix this error, you need to either manually change the field name in the control or change the field name in the table back to the original name and then set Access to track and automatically update changed field names throughout the database.

  To track and update changed field names, choose the Tools→Options command. On the General tab, mark the Track Name AutoCorrect Info and Perform Name AutoCorrect check boxes.

SEE ALSO *Expression, Field Name*

Events see Macros

Exiting Access

To exit Access, choose the File→Exit command or click the Access program window's Close box.

Exporting Data

You can export Access data to a variety of other file types, and to other Access databases. Exporting is useful for sending data to someone who doesn't have Access, and also for backing up data.

- You can export tables, queries, forms, and reports to Excel, HTML, text file, and other formats.

- You can also export tables and queries to dBASE, Lotus, Paradox, and ODBC database file formats.

- You can export reports to a Snapshot file format.

- You can export all database objects to other Access databases.

To export a database object:

1. Open the object group in the database window, and select the name of the object you want to export.

2. Choose the File→Export command.

3. In the Export *Object 'name'* To dialog box, navigate to the folder where you want to save the exported file.

4. Give the exported file a name in the File Name box, and select the export file type in the Save As Type box, then click Export.

Some file types will ask questions about how you want the data exported, and other file types (such as Excel) will create the new file with no input from you.

TIP   *If you're exporting a table to back it up, make a test export and then try to import the file back into your database. Some file types, such as text files, can be very difficult to import back into an Access database, even though you exported the file from your database. If a table contains fewer than 65,535 records, you can quickly back it up in an Excel file, and just as quickly re-import it if you need to. Better yet, create another Access database just for backup data and objects, and export your data and database objects to the backup database.*

SEE ALSO   *Report, Snapshot*

Expression

An expression is a formula that calculates a value or defines a criteria; you can use an expression in any database object to calculate new values or to specify which records should be displayed. You can type expressions yourself, or write them with the help of the Expression Builder.

Expression Builder

The Expression Builder (shown in Figure E-1) is an Access feature that helps you to build expressions by providing correctly spelled object names and correct expression syntax.

E

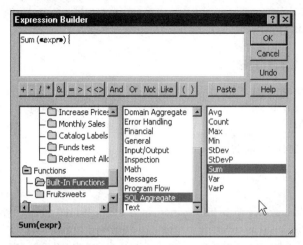

Figure E-1   The Expression Builder.

To open the Expression Builder:

• For a calculated field in a query, open the query in Design view and click the Build button on the Access toolbar (the Build button looks like a wand over three dots).

• For a calculated control in a form or report, click the control in Design view, click the Build button on the Access toolbar, and double-click Expression Builder in the Choose Builder dialog box.

To use the Expression Builder:

• Build the expression you want by double-clicking database field names, mathematical and logical operators, and functions, in the order that you want them to appear in the expression. As you double-click expression items and buttons, the items appear in correct syntax and spelling in the box at the top of the Expression Builder.

• To locate field names, double-click the plus symbol next to the object group in the left box. When a list of the objects in that group appears below the group name, click the name of the object. When a list of the fields in that object appears in the middle box, double-click a field name to add it to your expression.

• To locate functions, double-click Functions in the box on the left, and then click Built-In Functions. Click a function category in the middle box, and then double-click a function name in the box on the right to add the function to your expression. When the function appears in the expression, it includes placeholders for the arguments it requires—be sure you fill in the correct arguments.

- To delete part of an expression in the box at the top of the Expression Builder, select the characters and press Delete.

External Table

An external table is a table outside the open database which is used by the open database. It can be in another Access database or in an Excel file or text file.

SEE ALSO *Tables, Linking*

Field

A field is a category of information, such as Last Name or Fruit Type. Fields are displayed as columns in tables and queries, and as controls (of many types) in forms and reports. A field's data is always stored in a table, although it can be displayed in queries, forms, and reports.

Adding a Field

You can add new fields to your tables whenever you need to. To add a field:

1. Open the table in Design view.

2. Click in the first empty cell in the Field Name column, and type a field name. Make the field name short but easy to understand and spell. Good database practice is to avoid using spaces in field names.

3. In the Data Type column, select a data type that's appropriate for the data you'll store in the new field (shown in Figure F-1).

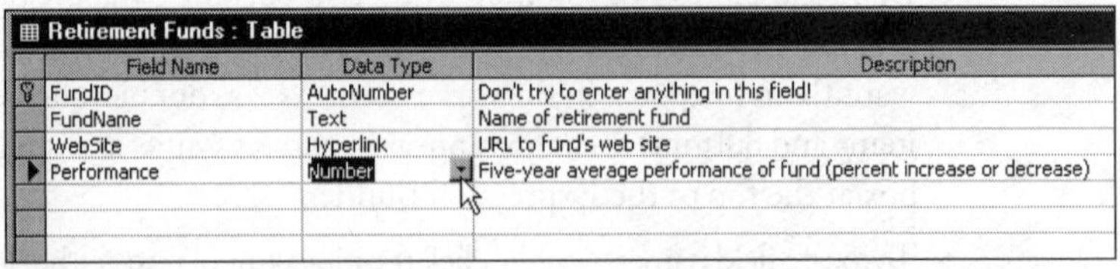

Field Name	Data Type	Description
FundID	AutoNumber	Don't try to enter anything in this field!
FundName	Text	Name of retirement fund
WebSite	Hyperlink	URL to fund's web site
Performance	Number	Five-year average performance of fund (percent increase or decrease)

Figure F-1   Selecting a data type for a new field.

4. In the Description column, you can type text that will appear in the Access status bar whenever the insertion point is in the field.

5. While the insertion point is in the new field row, set the field's properties in the Field Properties pane. The properties are different for each data type.

Deleting a Field

There are two ways to delete an entire field from a table:

- Open the table in Datasheet view, right-click the field name (the gray column heading), and click Delete Column.

- Open the table in Design view, click the row selector on the left side of the field you want to delete, and press Delete.

With either method, click Yes when asked if you're sure you want to permanently delete the selected field and all the data in the field.

NOTE   *If you are not allowed to delete the field, it's because the field is joined to a field in another table. Open the Relationships window, right-click the window, and click Show All to show all the relationships in the database. Then right-click the join line between the field you want to delete and any other tables, and click Delete.*

SEE ALSO   *Calculated Field, Data Types, Field Properties, Relationships*

Field Captions

Field captions are what the user sees in table Datasheet views of tables and queries, and in control labels in forms and reports. Changing a field caption won't affect your database structure or function.

To change a field caption in a table: open the table in Design view, and click in the field row in the upper pane. In the Field Properties pane, type the new caption in the Caption property box.

To change a field caption in a query: open the query in Design view. In the QBE grid, in the field's column, in the Field cell, type the new caption followed by a colon (:) on the left side of the field name, as shown in Figure F-2.

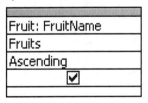

Figure F-2   **Fruit** is this query field's caption; **FruitName** is the field name.

NOTE   *If the field already has a caption applied in the table, that caption is used in the query field, and typing another caption followed by a colon does nothing unless the table field caption is erased.*

Field Description

A field description is text you type in the Description column in a table's Design view (shown in Figure F-3). A field's Description entry appears in the Access status bar whenever the insertion point is in that field in a table, form, or query. Field descriptions can be a good source of helpful information for someone entering or looking up data in the database.

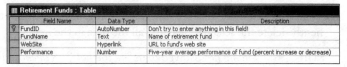

Figure F-3   Field descriptions in a table's Design view.

Field List

The field list is a list of all the fields in the underlying table or query for a form or report in Design view (Figure F-4 shows a field list for a form). You use a field list when you create bound controls on forms and reports. It normally appears by default when you open a form or report in Design view, but if it doesn't appear, you can show it by clicking the Field List button on the Design toolbar.

Figure F-4   A form's field list.

SEE ALSO *Controls*

Field Name

A field name is the name by which Access recognizes a field. It does not have to be identical to the user-friendly field caption that a field's column heading displays in Datasheet view. It is, however, the name you must use to refer to the field in expressions.

A field name has these requirements:

- Maximum length is 64 characters, including spaces.
- It cannot include these characters: ! . ` []

- It cannot begin with leading spaces.

- It cannot include control characters (ASCII values 0 through 31)

- It cannot include a double quotation mark (")

TIP   *It's bad practice to include spaces in field names because they can produce conflicts in VBA code, and if the database is ever moved to a SQL Server the fields will have to be renamed without spaces.*

A field name is not the same thing as a field caption. Captions are what the user of a database sees when they look at the Datasheet view of a table or query, and they can be as long, user-friendly, and intuitive as you like.

Sometimes you discover that a field name you chose is perhaps not the best for your purposes, and you want to change it. If you set the Track Name AutoCorrect feature before you change a field name, you can change a field name and Access will change all the references to that field name in database objects.

To change a field name: open the table in Design view. Edit the name in the Field Name column, and save the table.

NOTE   *To track and update changed field names, choose the Tools→Options command. On the General tab, mark the Track Name AutoCorrect Info and Perform Name AutoCorrect check boxes. Name AutoCorrect updates changed field names in database objects such as queries and forms, but not in expressions or Visual Basic for Applications code (you have to change names in expressions and VBA code manually).*

Field Properties

Field properties control what data can be entered in a field and how the data is displayed. You set field properties in the Field Properties pane in table Design view (shown in Figure F-5).

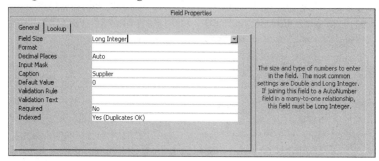

Figure F-5   The Field Properties pane for a field with the Number data type.

Which field properties are available for a field depends on the field's data type. Following are explanations of all the different field properties, as well as when and how to use them.

NOTE   *Before you set properties for a field, make sure that the correct field is selected. Click in the field row in the top half of the window, then set field properties.*

TIP   *For detailed information about a property, click in its property box and press F1.*

Field Size

The Field Size property determines how many numerals or characters can be entered in the field. Use the Field Size property to keep data entry more accurate. If the field stores phone numbers, for example, and you know that no phone number can be longer than 14 characters, enter **14** in the Field Size box.

TIP   *The default Text field size of 255 characters is the maximum you can set, and it reserves too much storage space for most Text fields. You can keep your database more compact by reducing the field size to no more characters than you know you'll need.*

Format

The Format property sets the display format for the field, and the available format choices depend on which data type is applied to the field.

Input Mask

The Input Mask property sets a pattern for data entered in the field. For example, you can format a field with an input mask for entering a telephone number. As shown in Figure F-6, when you type the first character in a field that has an input mask, punctuation marks and blank spaces display the structure for the entry (and the input mask will not let you leave an incomplete entry in the field). You don't type anything but the digits—the input mask supplies all the punctuation marks.

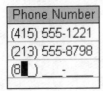

Figure F-6   An input mask for a telephone number field.

To create an input mask for a selected field, click in the Input Mask box and click the three-dots button that appears. Follow the steps in the Input Mask Wizard to create the input mask.

Caption

The caption is the field heading that the user sees, either in the table or in forms, queries, and reports created from the table. Good database practice calls for simple, one-word field names, but those kinds of field names (such as "Lname" or "$/#") are often not user-friendly and are sometimes quite confusing to someone who didn't create the database.

To make data clear and easy to understand, give each field an understandable caption, such as "Last Name" or "Price per Pound."

Default Value

The Default Value property enters a specific value in each new record, so you don't have to enter anything in that field unless the data is different. For example, if the majority of your Customers table's records will have Chicago in the City field, you can make Chicago the default value for the City field; and if a customer's address is in Bloomington instead of Chicago, all you have to do when entering a new record is select Chicago and enter **Bloomington** in its place.

Validation Rule

The Validation Rule property sets limits or conditions on the data that can be entered in the field. For example, you could require credit card expiration date entries to be later than the current date (so you know that the credit account is valid the day you take the order).

To create a validation rule, you enter a limiting expression in the Validation Rule text box.

Validation Text

If you established a validation rule for a field and someone enters data that breaks the rule, Access displays a standard error message. You can, however, write your own custom error message by entering the text in the Validation Text box.

TIP   *What do you do when you enter the wrong value and Access won't let you get out of it? First, try entering a valid value. If you don't know the correct data and want to get out of the record, press Esc.*

Required

The Required property makes an entry in the field required (or not). The default value is No; but if you set the property to Yes and then fail to enter a value in the field, you see a message telling you that an entry is required.

Allow Zero Length

The Allow Zero Length property, if set to Yes, allows you to enter a zero-length string ("") in a text, memo, or hyperlink field to distinguish it from a Null value.

Decimal Places

The Decimal Places property determines how many spaces are displayed to the right of the decimal point. This property affects how numbers and currency figures are displayed, but not their actual value. The Auto setting allows the Format property to determine the number of decimal places displayed.

Indexed

Indexes make searching and sorting operations go faster. In large databases, however, they also make table updates take longer and require more disk space for data storage. With the Indexed property, you can tell Access that you want to index a field in a table. No is the default choice. A field's indexing choices are:

- **No** No indexing.
- **Yes (Duplicates OK)** Indexes the field, but allows duplicate values to be entered in the field.
- **Yes (No Duplicates)** Indexes the field and prevents duplicate values from being entered in the field. Any field set as a primary key automatically has an index property of Yes (No Duplicates).

New Values

For fields with the AutoNumber data type, the New Values property determines whether the automatically assigned numbers are generated sequentially or at random. To make the AutoNumber field assign random numbers instead of sequential numbers, choose Random; if you don't have a reason for using random numbers, keep the default Increment setting for sequential number assignment.

IME Mode and IME Sentence Mode

IME is the Input Method Editor. These settings apply to East Asian and Japanese languages, and if you're not working in East Asian or Japanese languages, you should leave the default settings.

Unicode Compression

Unicode is a character-encoding standard that enables almost all the written languages in the world to be represented by a using a single character set. Unless you have a reason to change it, leave the default setting.

SEE ALSO *Validation Rules, Validation Text*

Field Selector

In Datasheet view for a table or query, field selectors are the gray heading boxes at the tops of the columns (fields). To select an entire field, click the field selector.

In a table's Design view, field selectors are the gray boxes on the left side of the Field rows. You click a field selector to select the entire field row when you want to delete or move a field in Design view. Also, when a field is designated the primary key for the table, the primary key icon is displayed in the field selector.

File Names

When you create a new database file or export data to another file, you need to give the file a name by entering a name into the File Name box in the File New Database or the Export As dialog box.

A file name can be up to 215 characters including spaces. All letters and numbers can be used in file names. Some symbols can be used, but not the symbols that follow:

\ / : * ? " < > |

File Properties

Access and other Office programs collect information about the files you create, including the file location, size, last date opened, and so forth. You can view this information about database files by choosing the File→Database Properties command.

Fill Color see Coloring

Filters

A filter is a set of criteria you apply to records in a table, query, or form to show a specific subset of those records, and to hide any records not meeting the criteria. Filtering locates and displays a group of records that have specific field entries in common. Filters are removed when an object is closed.

Filter By Form

A Filter By Form is for more complex filters, such as filters that use criteria operators instead of simply filtering on field entries. You can run a Filter By Form on a table, query, or form. To create a Filter By Form:

1. Open the datasheet or form you want to filter, and then click the Filter By Form button on the toolbar.

2. In the Filter By Form window, click in a field and type the criterion on which you want to filter. Figure F-7 shows a filter for fruits that cost more than $2.00 per pound.

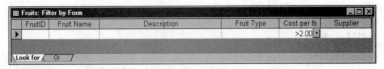

Figure F-7   A filter for complex criteria requires a Filter By Form.

3. Click the Apply Filter button on the toolbar, and your complex filter is applied.

TIP   *If you get lost in your filter criteria and the filter seems to be messed up, click the Remove Filter button; then create the correct filter.*

Filter By Selection

A Filter By Selection is very quick. It filters records based on a specific field entry. For example, you can filter a table of customer addresses to show only those from a specific state. To run a Filter By Selection:

1. Open the object (table, query, or form) you want to filter.

2. In the field on which you want to filter, click in any cell that contains the entry for which you want to filter (as shown in Figure F-8).

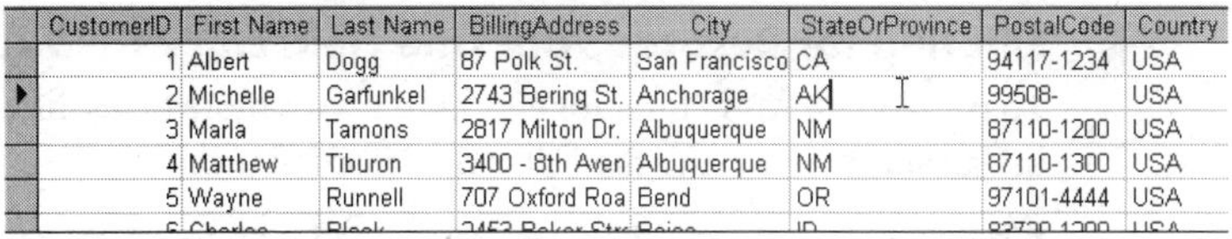

CustomerID	First Name	Last Name	BillingAddress	City	StateOrProvince	PostalCode	Country
1	Albert	Dogg	87 Polk St.	San Francisco	CA	94117-1234	USA
2	Michelle	Garfunkel	2743 Bering St.	Anchorage	AK	99508-	USA
3	Marla	Tamons	2817 Milton Dr.	Albuquerque	NM	87110-1200	USA
4	Matthew	Tiburon	3400 - 8th Aven	Albuquerque	NM	87110-1300	USA
5	Wayne	Runnell	707 Oxford Roa	Bend	OR	97101-4444	USA
6	Charles	Block	2453 Baker Stre	Boise	ID	83720-1200	USA

Figure F-8   This filter will display only records with **AK** in the StateOrProvince field.

3. On the toolbar, click the Filter By Selection button (it looks like a funnel with a lightning bolt).

The navigation area at the bottom of the datasheet window tells you the data are filtered.

You can also Filter By Selection for specific words or characters in a field. For example, in Figure F-9, the Filter By Selection will show only records in which the Description entry begins with the word **Pitted**.

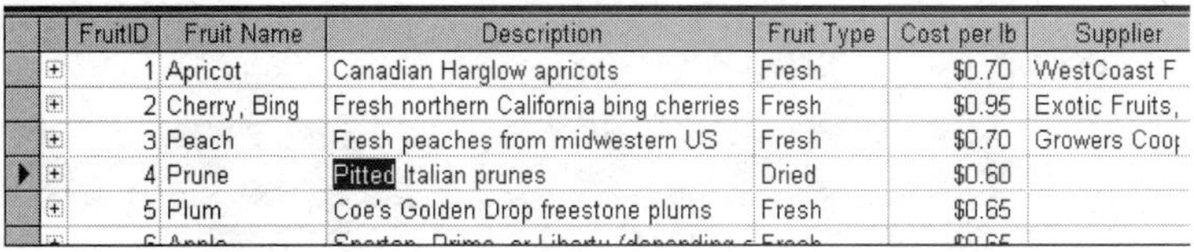

	FruitID	Fruit Name	Description	Fruit Type	Cost per lb	Supplier
⊞	1	Apricot	Canadian Harglow apricots	Fresh	$0.70	WestCoast F
⊞	2	Cherry, Bing	Fresh northern California bing cherries	Fresh	$0.95	Exotic Fruits,
⊞	3	Peach	Fresh peaches from midwestern US	Fresh	$0.70	Growers Coo
⊞	4	Prune	Pitted Italian prunes	Dried	$0.60	
⊞	5	Plum	Coe's Golden Drop freestone plums	Fresh	$0.65	
⊞	6	Apple	Spartan, Prima, or Liberty (depending c	Fresh	$0.65	

Figure F-9   This filter will display only records where the Description begins with **Pitted**.

To Filter By Selection for partial field entries: select the words or characters for which you want to filter in one cell, and then click the Filter By Selection button on the toolbar.

Filter Excluding Selection

To filter for all records except those with a specific field entry: click in a cell that contains the entry you want to exclude, or select the word or characters you want to exclude. Right-click the selection, and click Filter Excluding Selection.

Filter For

The Filter For shortcut menu command is another way to filter by selection. Right-click in any cell in the field on which you want to filter, and in the Filter For box on the shortcut menu, type the entire entry for which you want to filter.

Filtering for Records with One Field Entry AND Another

To run a quick AND filter for entries in two or more fields, filter each field in datasheet view using the Filter By Selection technique.

Filtering for Records with One Field Entry OR Another

An OR filter displays records that have either of two (or more) entries in a particular field. An example of an OR filter is a filter in a Customers table for customers in Vermont OR Virginia. To run an OR filter, you use a Filter By Form.

To create an OR filter:

1. Click the Filter By Form button on the toolbar. If you're filtering a table or query, the datasheet is replaced by a Filter By Form window that looks like the one in Figure F-10. If you're filtering a form, the datasheet is replaced by a Filter By Form window that looks like the one in Figure F-11.

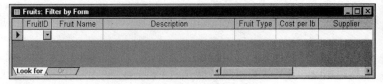

Figure F-10   The Filter By Form window for a table or query.

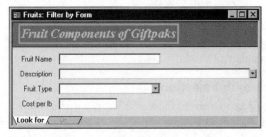

Figure F-11   The Filter By Form window for a form.

NOTE   *Access remembers previous filter criteria, so filter criteria may appear in the window. On the toolbar, click Clear Grid (the button with the red X) to remove all previous filter criteria.*

2. Click the Look For tab at the bottom of the Filter By Form window (if it's not already selected.)

3. Click in the field you want to filter, click the down arrow, and click the entry you want to filter for.

4. At the bottom of the Filter By Form window, click the Or tab. (The Or sheet is identical to the Look For sheet, so you have to check the tabs to be sure what sheet you're on.)

5. On the Or sheet, in the field you want to filter, click the down arrow and select the other entry for which you want to filter.

NOTE   *Another Or sheet has been automatically added to the window in case you'd like to add more OR criteria to your filter.*

6. On the toolbar, click Apply Filter.

The OR filter is applied, and your datasheet or form shows the filtered records.

Removing a Filter

To remove a filter, click the Remove Filter button on the toolbar (it looks like a funnel). You can also choose the Records→Remove Filter/Sort command.

Reapplying a Filter

To reapply the most recent filter, click the Apply Filter button on the toolbar (it looks like a funnel, and is the same button you clicked to remove the filter).

Filter Criterion Examples

Here are some more examples of common filter criteria:

TO	DO THIS
Filter on a single word	Select the entire word; then click Filter By Selection on the toolbar.
Filter on part of a word	Select the characters you want to filter on; then click Filter By Selection on the toolbar.
Filter on two or more fields—an AND filter	Select the words or characters in one field; then click Filter By Selection. In the filtered list, select the second criterion you want to filter on; then click Filter By Selection again. Repeat this process to add more AND criteria.

TO	DO THIS
Filter on a word that appears only at the beginning of an entry	Select the word at the beginning of an entry; then click Filter By Selection. Only records beginning with the selected word will be shown in the filtered list.
Filter on a word that appears anywhere in an entry	Select the word in the middle of an entry; then click Filter By Selection. All records containing the selected word anywhere in the entry will be shown in the filtered list.
Filter on a word that appears only at the filtered list	Select the word at the end of an entry; then click Filter By Selection. Only records ending in the selected word will be shown in the end of an entry.

SEE ALSO *Criteria Operators*

Finding a Database File

You can locate lost or misplaced database files using the Access Search tool. To use the Access Search tool, choose the File→Open command, click the Tools button, and choose the Search command. When Access displays the Search dialog box (shown in Figure F-12), enter the file name into the Search Text box. Use the Search In box to specify on which drives Windows should look. Use the Results Should Be list box to select Access Files. Then, click the Search button. To open a database file in the Results list, double-click it.

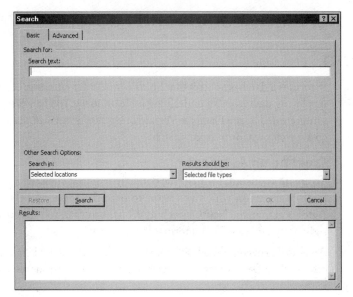

Figure F-12   The Basic tab of the Search dialog box.

TIP   *If you don't know the file name but know something about the*
           database's characteristics—such as what the database contains
           or who created the database—click the Advanced tab. Use its
           Property box, Condition box, and Value box to identify a file
           characteristic you can describe.

Finding Records

You can find specific records in a table, form, or query by using the Find tool.
You can find and display groups of records in a table, form, or query by
filtering.

SEE ALSO *Filters, Finding Specific Data*

Finding Specific Data

To locate a specific record when you know only part of an entry, such as a
street name, open the table, query, or form you want to search and click in
the field you want to search. Click the Find button on the toolbar (it looks
like binoculars), and fill in the Find tab in the Find And Replace dialog box.

TIP   *If you're searching for part of a field, such as a partial last name*
           or a street name in an address, be sure to select Any Part Of Field
           in the Match box.

71

Footers see Headers and Footers

Form

A form is a database object that holds controls for entering, editing, and displaying data from an underlying table or query. You can easily modify forms created by the Database Wizard or by the Form Wizard, and you can create your own forms from scratch.

Creating an AutoForm

To create an instant form: in the database window, click the name of the table or query on which you want to base the form, and then choose AutoForm from the New Object button on the toolbar. You can use the form right away, and modify and format it as much as you like.

An AutoForm contains all the fields in the underlying table or query. You can switch to Design view and delete the controls for any fields you don't want in the form.

NOTE   *If AutoForm creates a main form/subform, the subform is a blank subform control in the main form's Design view. You can't modify the subform—which is a good reason to use the Form Wizard to create forms with subforms.*

Creating a Form Using the Form Wizard

The Form Wizard is usually the best way to create a form, because the wizard does all the tedious work while allowing you some input on content and style. To create a form using the Form Wizard:

1. In the database window, in the Objects pane, click the Forms icon to open the Forms group.

2. Double-click Create Form By Using Wizard.

3. In the first wizard step (shown in Figure F-13), select the main table for the form in the Tables/Queries box. In the Available Fields list, double-click each field you want to include on the form. If you want to include them all, click the double-arrow button between the Available Fields and Selected Fields lists. (To remove a field from the Selected Fields list, double-click it.)

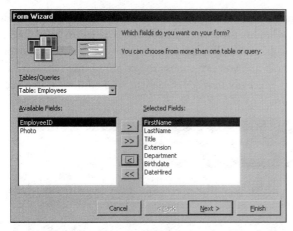

Figure F-13   Selecting fields for a form in the Form Wizard.

If you're creating a form based on two tables, select the second table in the Tables/Queries box, and add the fields you want to the Selected Fields list.

NOTE   *To create a form based on two tables, the tables must be related before you create the form.*

4. Click Next. If you're creating a table based on a single table or query, skip this step and go to step 5. If you're creating a form based on two tables, the next wizard step looks like the one in Figure F-14, and you decide which table provides the main form records and which table provides the subform records.

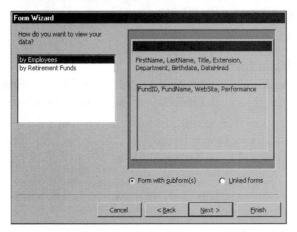

Figure F-14   The second wizard step for a two-table form.

5. In the next wizard step, choose a layout for the form. For a single-table form, Columnar is most common and is easiest to customize. In a main form/subform combination, shown in Figure F-15, the main form will be columnar and you can choose the layout for the subform. (Datasheet layout is usually best for displaying and editing related records in a subform.)

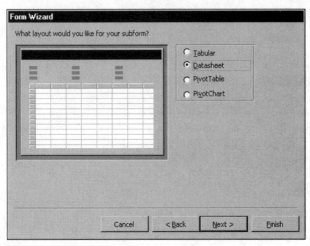

Figure F-15   Choose a layout for a main form/subform.

6. Click Next, and in the next wizard step, select a style.

7. Click Next, type a name for your new form (and subform, if you have one), and click Finish. Although a subform is contained in the main form, it's a separate form in the database.

SEE ALSO *Relationships*

Creating a Form Yourself

If you want to create your own switchboard form, or a form that displays only information (no records), the best way is to create the form from scratch.

To create a form from scratch: in the database window, in the Forms group, double-click Create Form In Design View. Add controls to the form grid from the Toolbox, modify the controls, and save the form.

TIP   *Large labels are a good way to display information on a form, and command buttons are good controls to use on a switchboard for opening other database objects.*

To create a form from scratch that can display records: right-click the gray box in the upper-left corner of the form window, and click Properties. In the Form properties sheet, on the Data tab, click in the Record Source property box. Click the arrow that appears, and select a table or query from the list of database objects. Then use the Field List and the Toolbox to add bound controls to the form.

Modifying a Form

No matter how a form was created, there are modifications that can make the form more efficient. For example, you can remove the navigation area from a subform, or remove scrollbars or record selectors.

To make modifications to a form's architecture: open the form in Design view. Right-click the gray box in the upper-left corner of the form window, and click Properties. On the Format tab of the Form properties sheet, change the settings in the appropriate property boxes.

TIP   *Switch between Form view and Design view as you make each change, to see what happens when you change a form's properties.*

Saving a Form

If you create an AutoForm or create a form from scratch, you're asked if you want to save it before you close it (click Yes, and give the form a name).

If you modify an existing form, you're asked if you want to save the changes before you close it. To be sure your changes are saved as you work, periodically click the Save button on the toolbar.

If you create a form using the Form Wizard, you're asked for a form name before the wizard is complete, and the form is saved when you click Finish.

Form Caption

A form caption is the title that appears in the form's title bar. By default the caption is the same as the name of the form, but you can display a different caption in the title bar.

To change a form's caption: open the form in Design view. Right-click the gray box in the upper-left corner of the form window, and click Properties. On the Format tab of the Form properties sheet, type a caption in the Caption property box.

Switching a Form to Datasheet View

You can show a form's records in Datasheet view, which looks like a table or query but shows only the fields that are included in the form.

To switch a form to Datasheet view, click the arrow on the View button on the toolbar, and choose Datasheet View.

Modifying Subforms

When you create a main form/subform by using the Form Wizard, you may want to modify the subform controls. For example, the subform has a navigation area which is unnecessary and may lead to confusion for anyone using the form to enter data or scroll through records, and when the subform has a datasheet layout, the columns may be the wrong width for the data.

To remove a navigation area from the subform: switch the main form to Design view, and right-click in the gray box in the upper-left corner of the subform. On the shortcut menu, click Properties. (The properties sheet should read Form in the title bar.) In the Form properties sheet, on the Format tab, click in the Navigation Buttons box and change the entry to No.

To resize the subform datasheet column widths: open the main form in Form view, and drag or double-click the right border of each column heading in the subform's datasheet. The new column sizes are saved when you save the form before closing it.

Setting the Tab Order

Tab order is the order in which the focus moves from control to control on a form when you press the Tab key.

To set tab order in a form, switch to Design view, click anywhere in the main form, and choose the View→ Tab Order command. In the Tab Order dialog box (shown in Figure F-16), be sure the Detail option button is selected (this is important if you click somewhere other than the Detail area before you click the Tab Order command). Rearrange the control names into the tab order you want: click the gray box to the left of a control name to select it, release the mouse button, and then drag the gray box for the selected control upward or downward to a new position.

F

Figure F-16   Setting a tab order.

Multi-Page Forms

A single form with controls separated onto separate pages usually is needed when a single-page form has too many controls for one convenient page. Figure F-17 shows a two-page form with tab controls. Pages are separated with tab controls, and displayed by clicking the page tabs at the top of the form.

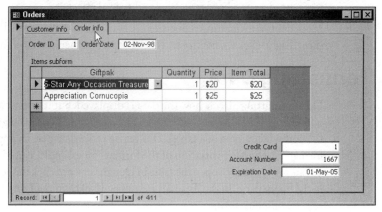

Figure F-17   A multiple-page form with tab controls.

SEE ALSO *Controls*

Form View

Form view is the view of a form that allows data entry and display, rather than form design and modification. Form view usually displays data from a table or query one record at a time, with added graphical elements for easier reading.

Format Painter

Format Painter is an easy way to copy formatting from one element to another (for example, from one control to another on a form). To use the Format Painter, select the formatted item you want to copy, then click the Format Painter button on the toolbar. Next, click the item to which you want to paste the copied formatting.

Formatting Controls

To format controls in forms and reports, open the form or report in Design view. Select the control(s) you want to format, and use the buttons on the Formatting toolbar to apply fonts, font sizes, font colors, fill colors and patterns, borders and border widths, and special effects.

More control formatting properties are available in the control's Properties sheet. Right-click the control and click Properties, then click the Format tab.

Formatting Data

Data formatting affects how the data is displayed, but it doesn't affect the underlying data value that Access uses for calculation. When you give a field the correct data type in a table's Design view, the data gets an appropriate format. **To choose a variation of the format** (for example, Euro instead of dollars for Currency): open the table in Design view and click in the field row in the upper pane. In the Field Properties pane, click in the Format box and select a different format.

The format you assign to a field in a table is carried into the queries, forms, and reports where the field is displayed.

You can make a field's display format different in a form or report without changing the format in the table. To change a field's format in a report or form, open the report or form in Design view, right-click the control, and click Properties. On the Format tab, in the Format property box, select the format you want for that control.

Formatting Toolbars

In Access, there are different Formatting toolbars for different object types, and a Formatting toolbar can only be displayed when the appropriate object is open in Design view. Each Formatting toolbar has all the buttons needed for formatting in the open object, and the buttons are unavailable unless an appropriate control or item is selected.

Formulas

Formulas are called *expressions* in Access. They're mathematical equations that calculate the data in your tables. They use any combination of functions, mathematical operators, data fields, and constant values. You can write expressions in calculated fields in queries and in calculated controls in forms and reports.

In a calculated field in a query, an expression (a formula) is written like the one shown in Figure F-18. On the left of the expression is the column caption, followed by a colon (:). On the right of the colon is the expression, in which field names are enclosed in square brackets. Expressions are calculated from left to right. In the expression shown here, the field caption is "10% Increase," and the expression multiplies entries in the Price field by a constant value of 1.1 to display a 10% increase in the price.

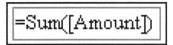

`10% Increase: [Price]*1.1`

Figure F-18   An expression in a calculated field in a query.

In a calculated control in a form or report, like the one shown in Figure F-19, an expression starts with an equal sign (=), and all field names are enclosed in square brackets. The expression shown uses a SUM function to sum the values in the Amount field. Because the field is an argument for the SUM function, the bracketed field name is enclosed in the function's parentheses.

`=Sum([Amount])`

Figure F-19   An expression in a calculated control in a report.

SEE ALSO *Calculated Controls, Expression, Functions*

Functions

Functions are pre-built formulas that make it easy to write complex expressions. Each function has a name that tells you what the function does, and most functions have arguments that tell the function what to calculate. The arguments are enclosed in parentheses.

To see a list of all the functions in Access, open the Expression Builder, double-click Functions in the left box, and then click Built-In Functions. Function categories are listed in the center box—click a category to see the functions in the right box.

If you double-click a function name, it appears in the upper box with placeholders for each of its arguments. Figure F-20 shows the Expression Builder with the Sum function selected.

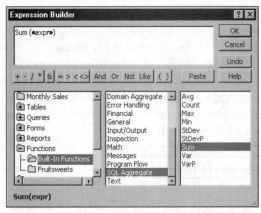

Figure F-20   A function in the Expression Builder.

NOTE   *If a calculated control returns the error #NAME?, it's probably because the name of the function is not recognized—it may be misspelled, or it may not be a function that Access recognizes.*

Graphic Objects see Picture Controls

Group

In a report, a group is a collection of similar details records that are grouped together for sorting and summarizing.

SEE ALSO *Report*

Group Footer

The section of a report where calculations or information that apply to a single group of records are displayed.

Group Header

The section of a report where labels and information that apply to a single group of records are displayed.

Grouping

In a grouped report, data is summarized in groups of entries from a specific field. For example, in a monthly sales report, details of sales over several months can be grouped by month, which makes the data much easier to read and understand.

SEE ALSO *Report*

Help

Within Access, you get help in two ways: from the Ask A Question box and from the Office Assistant. The Ask A Question box sits in the upper-right corner of your program window. To use it, type a word or phrase in the box, press Enter, and click a topic on the help topics menu that drops open.

The Office Assistant supplies the same kind of help that the Ask A Question box provides (but it doesn't keep a list of your questions). To use the Office Assistant, click the Office Assistant character. If the Office Assistant isn't already displayed, choose the Help→Show The Office Assistant command. Then type your question into the box provided and click Search.

Horizontal Pages see Page Orientation

HTML

HTML is the file format used in web pages. Access can create database objects called data access pages, which are HTML pages that look and work like Access forms.

SEE ALSO *Data Access Pages*

Hyperlinks

A hyperlink is colored and underlined text that you click to jump to an Internet or intranet web page or to another file or folder on your hard drive or network. An Internet hyperlink, called a URL, usually begins with "http://." A hyperlink to a file on your computer consists of the path to the file, formatted as a hyperlink.

You can store hyperlinks in table records, and you can add them as labels to forms.

To create a field for hyperlinks in a table, create a new field and give it a data type of Hyperlink. To enter hyperlinks in the table's records: open the table in Datasheet view, click in the cell where you want to enter the hyperlink, and choose the Insert→Hyperlink command. Use the Insert Hyperlink dialog box to create the hyperlink.

To create a label that's a hyperlink in a form, open the form in Design view and choose the Insert→Hyperlink command. Use the Insert Hyperlink dialog box to create the hyperlink. The hyperlink label appears in the upper-left corner of the form, and you can move it where you need it after it's finished.

TIP   *To change a hyperlink, right-click the hyperlink, point to Hyperlink, and choose the Edit Hyperlink command from the shortcut menu. Access displays a dialog box like the one you originally used to create the hyperlink. Use it to make your changes. To remove a hyperlink from a form, right-click the hyperlink in Design view, point to Hyperlink, and click Remove Hyperlink on the shortcut menu.*

SEE ALSO *Data Access Pages*

Image Control

An image control is a control that displays a picture or other graphical image unrelated to any specific tables or records. It's similar to an unbound object frame, but because it's designed to hold only pictures, it's faster to load.

SEE ALSO *Controls*

Images see Background Pictures

Importing Database Objects

If you've already created a great form or report in another database that you'd like to use in a new database, you don't have to re-create it from the ground up. You can import any database object from one Access database to another, and set new Record Source properties for the imported object in the new database.

To import objects from another Access database: choose the File→Get External Data→Import command. In the Import dialog box, select the database file from which you want to import objects, and click Import. In the Import Objects dialog box (shown in Figure I-1), select each object you want to import (click the tabs at the top of the dialog box to open different object groups). Click OK to import all the selected objects into the open database.

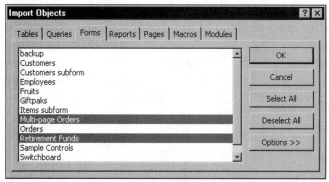

Figure I-1   Importing objects from another Access database.

You can also choose to import (or not) the relationships between objects, tables with data or without data, and queries as queries or as tables. To choose these options, click the Options button in the Import Objects dialog box, and mark or clear the check boxes and option buttons you want.

Importing Tables

You can copy data from another source (database, spreadsheet, and so on) into your open database by importing it as a table. Knowing how to import tables is an important efficiency tool. If data already exists in electronic form somewhere, you never want to re-type it if you can import it instead—importing is not only faster, but it reduces inaccurate data entry that can happen when data is typed.

The process of importing varies depending on the source from which you're importing.

Importing Tables from Other Access Databases

Importing tables from other Access databases is the same as importing objects from another Access database. Choose the File→Get External Data→Import command. In the Import dialog box, select the database file from which you want to import tables, and click Import. In the Import Objects dialog box, click the Tables tab, and select each table you want to import. Click OK to import all the selected tables into the open database.

You can also choose to import (or not) the relationships between tables, and import the tables with data or without data. To choose these options, click the Options button in the Import Objects dialog box, and mark or clear the check boxes and option buttons you want.

Importing Data from Excel

You can import data from Excel quickly and easily, because Excel and Access were designed to work together. Here are some things you should do to prepare the Excel file for an easy import:

- Set up the Excel file so that the table you want to import is alone on the worksheet (no extra entries anywhere).

- Format the data in each column with appropriate and specific number formatting. For example, make sure a column of telephone numbers is formatted as Text and not as General.

- Name the worksheet range you want to import (optional but helpful).

- Make sure the Excel data is clean; in other words, correct any inaccurate entries such as a letter character typed in a column of numbers.

To import an Excel table:

1. Choose the File→Get External Data→Import command.

2. In the Import dialog box, select Microsoft Excel in the Files Of Type box, then navigate to the Excel workbook from which you want to import a table.

3. Select the workbook name and click Import, then follow the steps in the Import Spreadsheet Wizard.

4. In the first wizard step, select the Show Named Ranges option if you named the worksheet range, and then select the range name. If you didn't name the worksheet range, select the Show Worksheets option and select the worksheet where the table is located (as shown in Figure I-2).

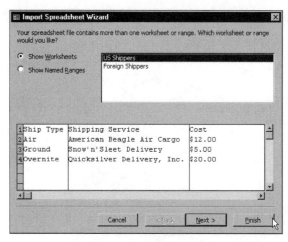

Figure I-2   Choose the worksheet or range name of the Excel table.

NOTE   *If there's only one worksheet in the workbook, and just a single range on the worksheet, you won't see the dialog box in Figure I-2.*

5. In the second wizard step, if the first row of the table is headings, mark the First Row Contains Column Headings check box.

6. In the third wizard step, select whether you want the table imported as a new table, or added to an existing table in the database.

   • If you want to import the data into an existing table, select the table name in the In An Existing Table box. The next wizard step will be the last, and you click Finish (don't rename the table).

7. If you import to a new table, the next wizard step (shown in Figure I-3), allows you to skip importing certain fields. To skip fields: click in the field column, and mark the Do Not Import Field (Skip) check box.

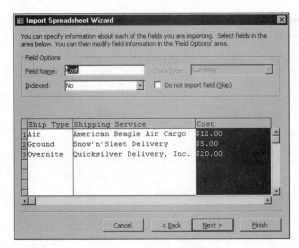

Figure I-3   Decide which fields to import, and check their data types.

TIP   *It's a good idea to click in each column and check the data type that's being imported with the field—you can't change the data type, but if you notice, for example, that a field of numbers is being imported as text, you should stop the import, open the Excel file and change the number formatting in the table, then start the import again.*

8. In the next wizard step, choose whether you want a primary key, and in the last wizard step, give the table a good database name.

Importing Data from Other Sources

Some other sources cannot be imported directly into Access (for example, some old FilePro database files cannot be imported). If a file type can't be directly imported into Access, you need to consult that program's documentation for exporting the data from that file to an intermediate file type, such as a text file or an Excel file, that can be imported into Access.

Many sources can be imported, however. (You can see the list of file types in the Import dialog box's Files Of Type box.) Most will use the Import Text Wizard to guide you through setting up the import.

SEE ALSO *Text Files*

86

Input Masks

An input mask is a field property that determines display format and limits the type of data that can be entered. Input masks make data entry faster and more precise. A common input mask is for a phone number field—a user enters the numbers (no punctuation), and the resulting entry is automatically punctuated and displayed properly.

Input masks can be set up for fields in tables and in form controls. The types of input masks the Input Mask Wizard offers depends on the data type of the field for which you are creating the input mask. Figure I-4 shows an input mask for entering dates in a form.

Figure I-4 An input mask for dates in a form control.

SEE ALSO *Field, Field Properties*

Joins

A join is a relationship between a field in one table and a field with a matching data type in another table. A *join line* is the graphical representation of the relationship that you see in the Relationships window. Figure J-1 shows two tables in the Relationships window, with a join line connecting them.

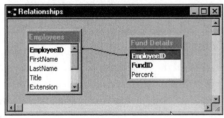

Figure J-1 Two related tables and the join line between them.

Choosing the Join Type

The *join type* controls how records are matched up when you run a query that includes two tables. When you gain expertise with Access queries, you'll want to change the join type occasionally.

When you create or edit a relationship, you can choose a different join type. To open the Edit Relationships dialog box, right-click the join line and choose Edit Relationships. In the Edit Relationships dialog box, click the Join Type button to open the Join Properties dialog box (shown in Figure J-2).

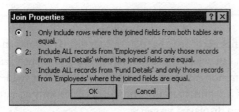

Figure J-2 Choosing a different join type.

The default join type (the first join type in the list) allows a query to display only records for which there is data in both tables. In other words, if you run a query on two tables, and a record in one table has no matching record in the other table, the unmatched record won't appear in the query recordset at all. The other two join types allow a query to show all records from one table, even if some of those records have no matching data in the other table.

Deleting Joins

Deleting a join deletes the relationship between two tables. Display the two tables in the Relationships window, right-click the join line, and click Delete.

NOTE   *Tables can be related in a query without being related in the Relationships window.*

SEE ALSO *Relationships*

Junction Table

A junction table is a table that provides a link between two tables that have a many-to-many relationship.

Figure J-3 shows three tables in the Relationships window. The outer tables have a many-to-many relationship with each other: each employee can be vested in many funds, and each fund can have many employee accounts. The central table is the junction table—it has a one-to-many relationship with each of the other two tables, and it provides added data about the joined records.

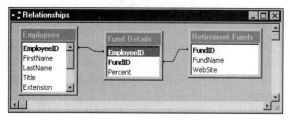

Figure J-3   The junction table in the center breaks a many-to-many
relationship into a pair of one-to-many relationships.

SEE ALSO *Data Types, Relationships*

Labels

A label is a control that displays informational text on a form or report. A label
may be tied to a bound control, or it may be used alone.

SEE ALSO *Controls*

Landscape Pages see Page Orientation

Linked Table

A linked table is a table stored outside the open database, but from which
the database can access records. An example of a linked table is a list in an
Excel file which you need to get data from periodically that's maintained by
another department in your company. You can create a *linked* table in your
Access database that allows your database objects to get current data from
that external Excel file, instead of creating a separate table in your database.

SEE ALSO *Tables, Linking*

List Box

A list box is a control that displays a list of values from which you can select
entries. Figure L-1 shows a list box.

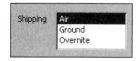

Figure L-1   A list box control.

SEE ALSO *Controls*

Lookup Fields

A lookup field is a field that looks up a list of values in another table or in a list of entries you create. A lookup field uses a combo box in the table to present the list of values for selection. Using a lookup field is quicker and guarantees no invalid or misspelled entries.

Creating Lookup Fields

You create a lookup field in a table by choosing the Lookup Wizard in the data type column for a field, and then following the wizard steps. The lookup field can look up entries in a field in another table or query, or it can look up entries on a static list you create. Figure L-2 shows a lookup field in a table that looks up entries in another table.

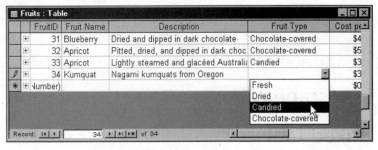

Figure L-2   A lookup field that looks up entries from a field in another table.

To create a lookup field that looks up entries in another table:

1. In Design view, click in the field in which you want to create a lookup list. In the Data Type column for that field, choose Lookup Wizard.

2. In the first Lookup Wizard step, click I Want The Lookup Column To Look Up The Values In A Table Or Query, and click Next.

3. The next wizard step asks for the name of the table or query where the lookup entries are located. Click the Tables, Queries, or Both option, depending on whether the lookup source is a table or query or you can't remember which. Click the table (or query) name where the source lookup field is located; then click Next.

4. The next wizard step asks for the name of the column whose values you want for the list. Double-click a column name in the Available Fields list to move that field into the Selected Fields list. Then click Next.

NOTE   *You can add more than one field to your lookup list—only one field's data will be saved in the lookup field, but another field can make it easier to identify the correct entry.*

5. In the next wizard step, if there's a primary key field, it will be hidden if you mark the Hide Key Column check box. If you only include one field in your lookup list, you won't see the Hide Key Column check box.

NOTE   *Even though you won't see the primary key entry in your lookup list, it's the primary key entry that's saved in the lookup field.*

6. If necessary, adjust the width of the column or columns so you can read the entries easily (either drag the right side of the column heading or double-click the right side of the column heading). Then click Next.

7. In the next wizard step, you can change the name of your lookup field if you want to. Then click Finish.

8. In the message that appears, click Yes. Access creates a relationship between the two tables so your lookup field will work.

To create a lookup field that looks up entries in a static list:

1. In Design view, click in the field for which you want to create a lookup list.

2. In the Data Type column, select Lookup Wizard.

3. In the first Lookup Wizard step, click I Will Type In The Values That I Want and then click Next.

4. The second Lookup Wizard dialog box appears (shown in Figure L-3), and you type the values that will appear on the list. Under Col1, type the first item that is to appear on the lookup list; then press Tab and type the next item. Continue until all the items are entered. When you have finished, click Next.

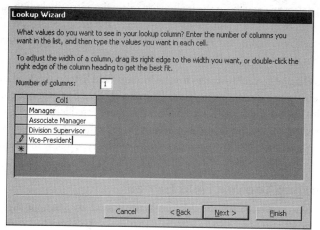

Figure L-3   Entering values for a static lookup field list.

5. In the next Lookup Wizard dialog box, you can change the field name if you want to. Then click the Finish button.

TIP   *You can create a multicolumn drop-down list by entering the number of columns you want in the Number Of Columns box and entering choices under each column. Only one of the columns will be stored in the field, but the other columns in the lookup list can help a user to identify the correct entry.*

Click the Lookup tab in the properties pane at the bottom of the Design view window. There you will see the properties for the lookup list you just created.

Using Lookup Fields

To use a lookup field to enter data, you first move the insertion point into the field. Then do one of two things:

• Click the arrow on the right side of the field, and select an entry from the list.

• Type the first letter of the entry you want. The first entry beginning with that letter appears. If there is more than one entry beginning with the same letter, you can type the first two or three letters of the entry.

Modifying Lookup Fields

What if you need to change the list after you've entered data in the table? You can change the field properties for the lookup field.

To change the entries on a static lookup list: on the Lookup tab in the field's properties pane, in the Row Source box, you can change the list of entries. To delete an entry from the lookup list, select the entry (including surrounding quote marks and following semi-colon), and press Delete. To add a new entry to the lookup list, type the new entry, surrounded by quote marks, and separate it from the other entries with a semicolon.

To change the column size for the lookup field list: on the Lookup tab in the field's properties pane, in the Column Widths box, you can change the width of each column. The column widths are listed left to right and separated by semicolons. Hidden columns (usually the ID or primary key field) have a width of 0". To change a column width, type a new measurement in inches, with decimals.

Sorting Lookup Field Entries

Looking up entries is much easier if the entries are sorted in alphabetical order. But quite often a lookup field that looks up entries in a table or query won't be sorted. You can sort a lookup field list like this:

1. On the Lookup tab in the field's properties pane, click in the Row Source box. Click the Build button that appears (the button with three dots).

2. A query window opens. In the QBE grid, in the field you want to sort, click in the Sort row and choose Ascending or Descending.

3. Close the query window, and click Yes when you're asked if you want to save.

4. Save the table, and switch to Datasheet view to test the lookup field.

Lookup Lists

A lookup list can be either a lookup field in a table or a combo box or list box control in a form. The lookup list can look up entries in a field in another table or query, or offer a static (unchanging) list of entries that you set up when you create the control or field.

SEE ALSO *Controls, Lookup Fields*

Lookup Wizard

The Lookup Wizard helps you to create a lookup field in a table. You choose the Lookup Wizard from the list of data types in a table's Design view.

SEE ALSO *Lookup Fields*

Macros

A macro is a set of one or more actions that each perform a particular operation, such as opening a form or printing a report. Macros are an easy-to-use technique for automating your database without using any programming code.

Creating Macros

You create a macro by opening a new macro window, choosing a macro action, and entering the arguments, or information, for the macro. Here's an example of a macro that opens a report:

1. In the database window's Objects bar, click Macros. With the Macros group open, click the New button in the database window toolbar. A new macro window opens.

2. In the Action column, choose an action for the macro to perform (to create a macro that opens a report, choose the OpenReport action).

3. After you choose an action, the Action Arguments pane shows the arguments for that macro. Figure M-1 shows the arguments for the OpenReport action.

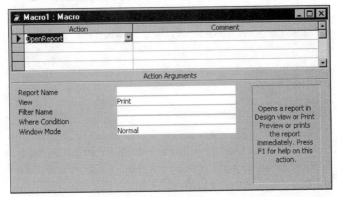

Figure M-1   A new macro window.

4. Click in the Report Name box, click the arrow that appears, and choose a report from the list. All the reports in the database are listed—select the one you want.

5. In the View box, you can choose Print (to print the report immediately), or Design or Print Preview to open the report before you send it to the printer.

6. Click the Save button on the Access toolbar, and give the macro a recognizable name.

The completed macro can be attached to form controls and custom toolbar buttons.

Modifying Macros

To modify a macro, open the Macros group, click the name of the macro, and click the Design button on the database window toolbar. In the macro window, click in the macro name row, and make any changes you need in the macro arguments.

Deleting Macros

To delete a macro, select the macro name in the database window's Macros group, and press Delete.

Saving Macros

To save a macro, click the Save button on the Access toolbar while the macro window is open and active.

Running Macros from Controls

You can attach a macro to a control so that the macro runs when a specific control event occurs, such as clicking, double-clicking, or exiting the control. To attach a macro to a control event:

1. In Design view, right-click the control and click Properties.

2. In the Properties sheet, on the Event tab, locate the event to which you want to attach the macro. The Event tab for a text box control is shown in Figure M-2.

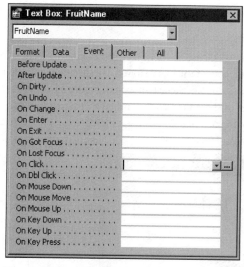

Figure M-2   The Event tab for a text box control in a form.

3. Click in the event box, click the arrow that appears, and select the macro name from the list.

TIP   *To learn more about a specific event, click in the event box and press F1 to open a help window about the event.*

Running Macros with Keystrokes

To run a macro with keystrokes, add the macro action and keystroke to a macro named AutoKeys.

SEE ALSO   *AutoKeys*

Macro Arguments

Macro arguments provide the information a macro action needs to perform the procedure you want. To learn more about a specific macro argument, choose a macro action, and then click in the argument's box in the Action

Arguments pane. A brief explanation of the argument appears in the panel on the right side of the Action Arguments pane. Press F1 to open a help window and get in-depth help about the action and all of its arguments.

Startup Macros

A startup macro runs when the database opens. A common startup macro opens a switchboard form for a database when the database opens.

Any macro saved with the name **AutoExec** is a startup macro. If you want to run more than one action as a startup macro, create each of the actions in the macro window for the macro named AutoExec.

Macro Events

A macro event is any database activity that triggers a macro. When you attach a macro to a control, you set the macro to run at a specific event, such as when the control is clicked, double-clicked, or exited. Figure M-3 shows the Event tab on the Properties sheet for a command button control. If you want the macro to run when the command button is clicked, you select the macro name in the On Click box.

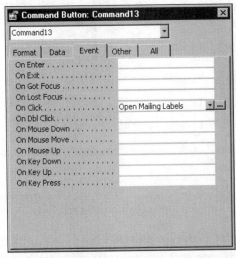

Figure M-3   Macros are set to run when specific events occur.

Macro Groups and Macro Names

A macro group is a collection of related macros stored together under a single macro name, such as AutoKeys. You create a macro group by displaying the Macro Name column (choose the View→Macro Names command). The Macro Name column is for names of macros in the macro group. Figure M-4 shows an AutoKeys macro group with two macros in it.

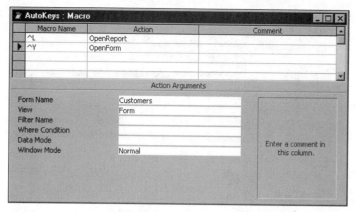

Figure M-4   The Macro Name column shows the names of the macros in a macro group.

Removing a Macro from a Control

To remove a macro from a control, so that no control event can trigger the macro, right-click the control in Design view and click Properties. On the Event tab in the Properties sheet, select the macro name and press Delete.

Magnification see Zoom

Mailing Labels

One of the very useful reports you can produce in Access is mailing labels. The Label Wizard does all the work for you, with a bit of input from you about the type of label you're creating and the source of your data. To create mailing labels in Access:

1. In the database window, in the Reports group, click the New button.

2. In the New Report dialog box, choose the table or query that contains the names and addresses for your labels, and then double-click Label Wizard.

3. In the first wizard step (shown in Figure M-5), select the type of label you're printing. Pay attention to the Unit Of Measure and Label Type options, because the options you select determine the products you see listed in the What Label Size Would You Like? list. Avery 5160 is a very common mailing label—to find it, click the English option, the Sheet Feed option, and Avery in the Filter By Manufacturer box.

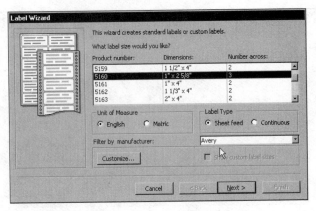

Figure M-5   Finding a commercial label type.

4. Click Next, and select a Font Name, Font Weight, and Font Size for your labels. You want the font to be large enough to be easily read, but small enough to fit on the label size you're using.

5. Click the Next button, and then lay out the data on the labels (as shown in Figure M-6). To insert a field, double-click it in the Available Fields list. To insert a space or a comma, type it in position between the fields. To start a new line, press Enter.

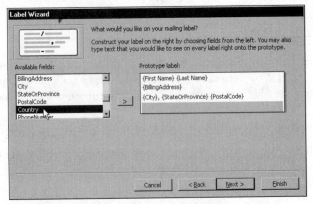

Figure M-6   Laying out a mailing label.

6. Click Next, and select a sort field. For bulk mailings, which must be sorted by postal code, choose a postal code field.

7. Click Next, give the labels report a name, and click Finish.

The finished report is ready to print (be sure you've loaded the labels you specified in step 3 into the printer).

You can run this report every time you need labels from this data source, and the data will be current every time you run it (because that's the nature of Access reports). To print the labels in the future, put labels in your printer, open the Reports tab in the database window, right-click the labels report name, and choose Print on the shortcut menu.

Main Forms see Form

Main Switchboard see Switchboard

Many-to-Many Relationship

A many-to-many relationship is a relationship between two tables in which each table can have many related records in the other table. Figure M-7 shows an example of a many-to-many relationship.

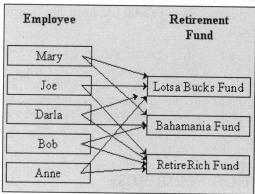

Figure M-7   Records in each table can have many related records in the other table.

Tables with a many-to-many relationship can be joined through an intermediate table, called a *junction table*, which breaks the many-to-many relationship into a pair of one-to-many relationships.

SEE ALSO *Junction Table, Relationships*

Margins

To set the margins for printed pages in a database object, open the object, and choose the File→Page Setup command. On the Margins tab, type measurements (in inches) for the Top, Bottom, Left, and Right margins.

Microsoft Office User Specialist

Microsoft certifies Access users who can pass a test as a Microsoft Office User Specialist, and in the parlance of Microsoft, these people then become MOUS certified. You don't learn anything new by becoming a MOUS certificate holder, but if you're in a career or an organization where certification delivers benefits, you should know that these tests are relatively straightforward to prepare for and pass.

Your first step is to learn what material you need to know to pass the test you want to take. You can get a summary of the test material from Microsoft's web site at www.microsoft.com. Just visit the web site and search on the phrase:

Microsoft Office User Specialist (MOUS) Access 2002 Exam Objectives

After you know what you need to know in order to pass the test, practice every task or skill a few times. You don't need a special study test or a class. After you've prepared, take the test at a local testing center. You can learn about any local testing centers from the local telephone directory or from the Microsoft web site.

TIP   *Perhaps the most important skill for passing a MOUS test is knowing how to use the Help files. You can't rely on this tool to answer every question the test asks—there isn't time—but as long as you're comfortable using the Help files, you should have time to ask a question or two you can't answer on your own.*

SEE ALSO *Help*

Mouse Selection Problems

There are a few intricacies to selecting controls on forms and reports. When you select a control and then click in it, so the insertion point flashes in the control, you won't be able to move or resize the control until you click away from it and then click it again to select it.

If you have problems selecting and moving a group of controls, select the group, and then position the mouse pointer over any of the selected controls so that you see the move pointer (the open-hand symbol). Then you can drag the selected group.

Moving Controls on Forms and Reports

To move a control on a form or report, click the control to select it (the selected control will have handles around its perimeter). Then position the mouse pointer over the control so that the mouse pointer becomes an open-hand symbol, and drag the control with the open-hand pointer to move it.

To move a control separately from its label, or to move a control's label separately from the control, click the control or label to select it. Position the mouse pointer over the large handle in the upper-left corner of the control or label, and when the mouse pointer becomes a hand with one finger pointing, you can drag the control or label by dragging the large handle. Figure M-8 shows both the open-hand symbol and the hand with one finger pointing.

Figure M-8 The open-hand pointer moves a control and its label; the hand with one finger pointing moves the control or label alone.

Moving Fields

In a table or query, you can rearrange columns in Datasheet view by selecting and dragging the column header. Moving a column in Datasheet view doesn't affect the arrangement of the fields in Design view.

To move fields in a table's Design view: click the gray row selector to select the field row, then drag the row selector to a new position in the list of fields.

To move fields in a query's Design view: in the QBE grid, click the gray bar above the field column you want to move. Then drag the gray bar left or right to reposition the field in the grid.

TIP   *When you want to sort a query by more than one field, you'll need to move the fields in the grid. Query fields are sorted left to right according to their position in the QBE grid. In addition to assigning a sort order in each field's Sort row, you need to position the sorted fields in hierarchical sort order from left to right.*

Multiple-Page Forms see Controls

Multiple-Tab Forms see Controls

Navigation Area

The navigation area is the area at the bottom of a form, report, table, or query window where you can click scroll buttons to select specific records. A form navigation area is shown in Figure N-1. The buttons and box from left to right are: First Record, Previous Record, active record number, Next Record, Last Record, and New Record. To the right of the buttons is the total number of records in the underlying table or query.

Figure N-1   A navigation area in a form.

NOTE   *In a report, the navigation area displays pages instead of records.*

Navigation Buttons in Subforms

In a form with a subform, both the main form and subform have navigation areas. This can lead to confusion if the subform is at the bottom of the main form and the two navigation areas are stacked on top of one another. It's usually good form design to remove the navigation area from a subform and let the user rely on scrollbars to move between records in a subform.

SEE ALSO *Form*

Objects Bar

The Objects bar is the vertical bar on the left side of the database window, from where you can open each group of objects (tables, forms, queries, reports, pages, macros, and modules).

Office Assistant see Help

Option Button

An option button is a control in a form for entering a value in a specific field. It functions as a Yes/No control when it's not part of an option group.

SEE ALSO *Controls*

Option Group

An option group is a group of option buttons that work together to provide a limited selection of data entry choices.

SEE ALSO *Controls*

OR Filter

An OR filter is a filter that finds records that meet one criterion OR another. An example of an OR filter is one that filters a Customers table for addresses that are in Montana OR Wyoming. Another example is a query that displays records of product orders that are less than $100 OR greater than $5000 (this query would hide records in which orders were in between $100 and $5000).

SEE ALSO *Filters*

Page Footer

A page footer is an area for text and/or graphics that appear at the bottom of each page in a report or form. Page footers often contain calculated controls for page numbers and page totals.

To add a page footer to a form or report, open the object in Design view and choose the View→Page Header/Footer command.

Page Header

A page header is an area for text and/or graphics that appear at the top of each page in a report or form. Page headers often contain column headings, logos, and so forth.

To add a page header to a form or report, open the object in Design view and choose the View→Page Header/Footer command.

Page Numbers

You can add page numbers to a report by creating a calculated control and entering the proper expression. A variety of built-in page number expressions are available, which saves you the trouble of writing them on your own. If you need to add or change a page numbering control in a report, here's how:

1. Open the report in Design view, and in the report's page footer, create an unbound text box control.

2. Click the text box control to select it, and then click the Build button on the Access Report Design toolbar (it's the button that looks like a wand over three dots).

3. In the Choose Builder dialog box, double-click Expression Builder.

4. In the Expression Builder (shown in Figure P-1), type an equal sign in the top box. Then click Common Expressions in the left box, and click a specific expression in the center box. Double-click the expression that appears in the right box.

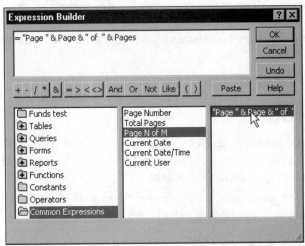

Figure P-1   Creating page numbers in the Expression Builder.

5. Drag to select the entire expression in the top box, and press Ctrl+C to copy it. Click OK to close the Expression Builder.

6. Double-click in the text box control, and press Ctrl+V to paste the expression. Move, resize, and format the control to look the way you want it to.

Page Orientation

Access will print your pages in either a portrait (vertical) orientation or a landscape (horizontal) orientation. To change the current orientation of the open object, choose the File→Page Setup command, click the Page tab, and then click either the Portrait or Landscape button (shown in Figure P-2).

Figure P-2   The Page tab of the Page Setup dialog box.

Palette

A palette is a small dialog box of choices that drops down when you click some toolbar buttons, such as the Fill/Back Color and Line/Border Color buttons. Palettes can be dragged away from the toolbar to "float" in the Access window, so you can use them repeatedly without having to open them each time. Figure P-3 shows the Font/Fore Color palette.

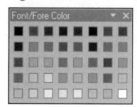

Figure P-3   Palettes can be dragged away from the toolbar for more convenient access.

Parameter

A parameter is the criterion that is temporarily written in a query when a user enters the information that a parameter query asks for.

If you run a query or report and see an unexpected Enter Parameter Value dialog box like the one shown in Figure P-4, the most likely problem is that a field name in a calculated field expression is misspelled or unrecognized. The unrecognized field name is shown in the dialog box so you can find and fix the problem in the query's Design view.

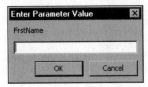

Figure P-4   The Enter Parameter Value dialog box appears when a field name is unrecognized.

SEE ALSO *Queries*

Password Protecting a Database

You can protect a database from being opened by unauthorized users by setting a password for the database. To set (or delete) a password, the database must be open for exclusive use.

CAUTION *If you forget the password for a database, you cannot open the database or get help from Access to recover the password.*

To password-protect a database:

1. Close the database, and then choose the File→Open command. In the Open dialog box, click the arrow next to the Open button, and click Open Exclusive.

2. Choose the Tools→Security→Set Database Password command. In the Set Database Password dialog box, type your password in both the Password and Verify boxes.

When anyone next opens the database, Access will ask for the password before the database will open.

To remove a password:

1. Choose the File→Open command. In the Open dialog box, click the arrow next to the Open button, and click Open Exclusive.

2. Enter the password to open the database.

3. Choose the Tools→Security→Unset Database Password command. In the Unset Database Password dialog box, type the password and click OK.

When anyone next opens the database, the database will open without a password.

Pasting

After you cut or copy an item, you can use a number of techniques to paste it elsewhere. You can press Ctrl+V, choose the Edit→Copy command, or click the item in the Office Clipboard task pane. You can also right-click where you want to paste the item, and click Paste in the shortcut menu.

TIP   *To show the Office Clipboard task pane, choose the Edit→Office Clipboard command.*

NOTE   *The Office Clipboard task pane won't show copied controls—you must use a different technique to paste controls.*

SEE ALSO *Copying Data and Formulas*

Picture Controls

You can add pictures, such as company logos, to forms and reports, and you can add a picture as a background to a form or report. When a picture is used in the background, all the other controls sit on top of the background picture. When a picture is used in a control, the picture sits in the foreground of the form or report along with all the other controls.

SEE ALSO *Background Picture, Controls*

Pictures in Tables see Bound Object Frame

Portrait Pages see Page Orientation

Previewing Reports

To preview a report before printing, click the report name in the database window and click the Preview button on the database window toolbar. To preview a report after making changes in Design view, click the View button on the Access toolbar.

Primary Key

A primary key is one or more fields in a table whose values uniquely identify each record. You select those fields in Design view and set them as the primary key by clicking the Primary Key button on the toolbar. To unset a primary key, select the primary key fields in Design view (the field rows marked with the key symbol) and click the Primary Key button. Figure P-5 shows a field in Design view set as the primary key.

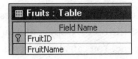

Figure P-5   The primary key field is marked with a key symbol in the field's row selector.

Primary Table

In a one-to-many table relationship, the table on the "one" side of the relationship is called the *primary table*. The table on the "many" side is called the *related table*.

Print Queue

Windows shows a print queue, or line, of the documents waiting to print on a printer if you click the Start button, point to the Settings command, click the Printers command, and then double-click the printer (see Figure P-6).

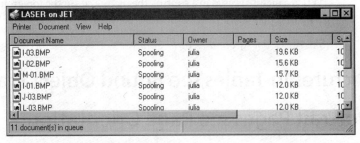

Figure P-6   A printer window.

Depending on your system privileges, you may be able to delete documents from the printer queue or to move documents backwards or forwards in the queue. To delete a file, right-click the file and choose Cancel from the shortcut menu. To move a document forwards or backwards in the queue, right-click the document, choose Properties from the shortcut menu and adjust the priority.

Printing

You can print table and query datasheets for a quick printout of data. When you want a professional, easy-to-read summary of data, you can create and print a report. You can also create and print a blank form for people to fill out on paper.

Printing Tables and Queries

Sometimes you need to see a concise list of the data in a table or query—you don't want it pretty, you just want it complete and fast. To print all or some of the records in a table or query, in datasheet format:

1. Open the table or query you want to print. It's a good idea to sort your table before you print it, so the printout is logical for the reader.

2. If you want to print only some of the records, drag the record selector boxes on the left to select those records. If you want to print the entire table, there is no need to select anything.

3. Choose the File→Print command, and in the File Print dialog box:
   - Click the All button to print the entire table (regardless of which records are selected).
   - Click Selected Record(s) to print only selected records.
   - If the table is very long and you only need to print the records that fit on specific pages, click the Pages option, and enter page numbers in the From and To boxes. (Before you do this, choose the File→Print Preview command and take a look at how the records are broken into pages, then make a note of the page numbers that contain the records you want to print.)

Printing Reports

The quickest way to print an entire report is to print it directly from the database window, without opening it first. In the database window, in the Reports group, right-click the name of the report and click Print on the shortcut menu.

If you want to print just part of a report, double-click the report's name to open it, and use the navigation area at the bottom of the report window to page through the report and decide which pages you want to print.

Choose the File→Print command. In the Print dialog box, click the Pages option, enter the number of the first page to print in the From box and the last page to print in the To box, or click the All option to print the entire report.

SEE ALSO *Report*

Printing a Blank Form

Why print a blank form? To give others a piece of paper to fill out, which you enter into the database at your convenience.

You can create a blank form by making a copy of the form you use to enter data. Remove all field references from the controls (delete the field name from each control). Remove the record source (in the Form properties sheet, on the Data tab, delete the object name in the Record Source box). You can resize the blank controls to make them large enough for handwriting when the form is printed.

Choose the File→Print Preview command to check the page before printing, and choose the File→Print command to print the form.

SEE ALSO *Form*

Protection see Password Protecting a Database

Queries

A query is a request for specific information, such as "Which products do our customers in Alaska order the most?" Queries enable you to focus on the specific data you need for your current task. A query's recordset can be drawn from multiple related tables, can have several filters applied, and can include calculated fields.

By using queries, you can examine your data in any way you can think of. You can choose the tables, fields, and records that contain the information you want to see, summarize, or calculate; you can sort that data to organize it; and you can create reports and forms that show just the information you choose (always the most current information). You can also send queried data to Excel to perform more extensive calculations.

The result of a query is called a *recordset*. A query recordset is not stored in the database (and, therefore, does not take up space on your hard disk); instead, it's created each time you run the query and dissolved each time you close the query. This saves hard disk space and ensures that your query displays only the most current data. If you're querying data from a table someone else on your network keeps updated, you won't know when data in the table has changed, but a query will always give you data that's current as of the moment you run the query.

You can use *action queries* to make large-scale changes to the data in a table. A Make-Table query can create a new table from the data in a query. A Delete query can delete queried records from a table. An Update query can update a table with changes to queried records. An Append query can add a set of queried records to another table.

The first step in creating a query is to decide what information you want to see. Next, you determine what tables the data are stored in, and then either build the query in Design view or use the Query Wizard.

Creating a Query Using the Wizard

The Query Wizard can help you create a query by asking you for the tables and fields you want to include. If you want the wizard to create a query from multiple tables, you must create the table relationships in the Relationships window before you use the Query Wizard. To create a query using the Query Wizard:

1. In the database window, in the Queries group, double-click Create Query By Using Wizard.

2. In the first wizard step, shown in Figure Q-1, select a table in the Tables/Queries box. In the Available Fields list, double-click each field you want to add to the query. If you want to add fields from other tables, to create a multiple-table query, select each table in the Tables/Queries box, and double-click the fields in the Available Fields list to add them to the Selected Fields list.

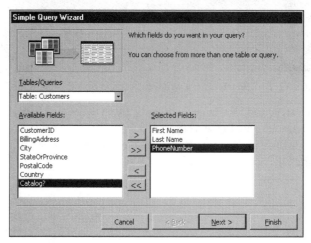

Figure Q-1   The first wizard step asks for the tables and fields you want to query.

NOTE   *If you include two tables that aren't already related in the Rela-*
tionships window, the wizard tells you to create the relationship
and then restart the wizard.

3. In the next wizard step, give the query a recognizable name and click
   Finish.

Creating a Query in Design View

Design view is an easy way to create queries, whether from a single table or
from multiple tables.

To create a single-table query in Design view:

1. In the database window, in the Queries group, double-click Create Query
   In Design View. A new query window and the Show Table dialog box
   appear.

2. In the Show Table dialog box (shown in Figure Q-2), click the table you
   want, click Add, and click Close to close the Show Table dialog box. The
   table is added to the table pane of the query window.

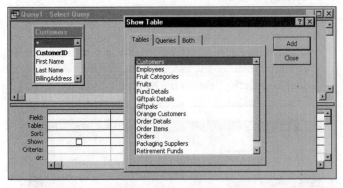

Figure Q-2   A new query window and the Show Table dialog box.

3. Next, you add the table fields you want to the query's QBE (Query By
   Example) grid. In the table pane, double-click each field name you want
   to include in the query. As you double-click field names, they appear in
   the QBE grid, shown in Figure Q-3.

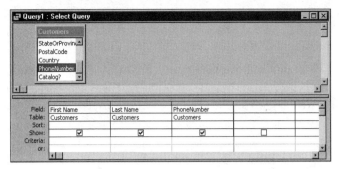

Figure Q-3 Double-clicked field names are added to the QBE grid.

4. On the Access toolbar, click the View button to switch to Datasheet view. The query runs, and the results will look like a table. You can sort on any column to make more sense of the data.

NOTE   *If a field in your QBE grid isn't showing up in the query datasheet, make sure the field's Show box (in Design view) is marked. If you accidentally clicked it and cleared it, the field will be hidden in the datasheet.*

Creating a multiple - table query in design view

To query data from more than one table, the tables must be related, but you don't have to create a permanent relationship in the Relationships window. The tables you want to use in a query can be related temporarily in the query window. Figure Q-4 shows a Design view of a three-table query, with a field from each table and a calculated field that concatenates names.

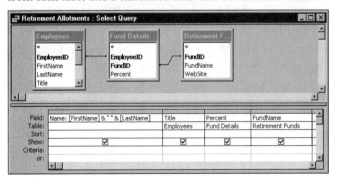

Figure Q-4 A three-table query in Design view.

NOTE   *The only requirement for relating two tables in a query is that they share common data in fields with the same data type and size (just like related tables in the Relationships window).*

TIP   *If the two tables you want to query won't join, see if they have a many-to-many relationship. If so, you'll need to create a junction table to join them.*

To create a multiple-table query:

1. In the database window, in the Queries group, double-click Create Query In Design View. A new query window and the Show Table dialog box appear.

2. In the Show Table dialog box, double-click each table name you want to add. Then close the Show Table dialog box. The tables are added to the Table pane.

3. Be sure the tables are joined—if they are, join lines appear between them. If the tables are permanently joined in the Relationships window, they'll be joined when you add them to the query. If the tables are not joined automatically in the query, create a relationship by dragging a field name from one table and dropping it on the matching field name in the other table.

4. Double-click the field names you want to include in the query to add them to the QBE grid.

5. Click the View button on the Access toolbar to switch to Datasheet view. The query displays the recordset for your query.

Modifying Queries

To modify an existing query, open the query in Design view. Make any changes you need, such as adding or deleting fields, entering criteria, and creating calculated fields, and then click the Save button on the Access toolbar to save your changes.

To add a field, click the field name in the Table pane. To remove a field, click the gray bar above the field name in the QBE grid, and press Delete.

To enter criteria, type criteria operators in the field's Criteria row in the QBE grid.

To create a calculated field, enter the expression in the Field row in a blank column in the QBE grid.

To add another table to the query, right-click in the Table pane and click Show Table. In the Show Table dialog box, select the table name you want and click the Add button. When you've added all the fields you want, click the Close button.

Saving a Query

To save an open query, click the Save button on the Access toolbar.

Crosstab Query

Some data is difficult to read in a list format because so much information is presented. Loan tables, for example, are traditionally displayed in a crosstab format, with loan amounts down the left side of the table and interest rates across the top. Payment amounts for a given loan amount at a specific interest rate can be looked up in the center of the table. You can create *crosstab queries* in Access if you need to present a similar kind of data.

To create a crosstab query that combines data from two or more tables, you first need to create a select query that combines the data you want, and then create the crosstab query from that select query. To create a crosstab query from a single table, you don't need to create a select query first. To create a crosstab query:

1. In the database window, in the Queries group, click the New button. In the New Query dialog box, double-click Crosstab Query Wizard.

2. The wizard starts and the first wizard step appears (shown in Figure Q-5). In the first wizard step, choose the query on which you'll base the crosstab query (click an option to show the tables or the queries or both).

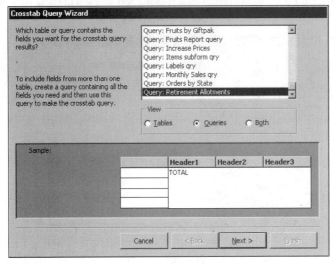

Figure Q-5   Choose the underlying table or query.

3. In the second wizard step, double-click the field you want listed down the side as row headings. In this example, shown in Figure Q-6, we want names listed down the left column, so double-click Name.

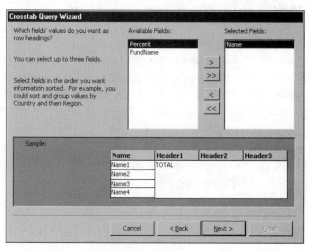

Figure Q-6   Choose the field for row headings.

4. In the third wizard step, shown in Figure Q-7, click the field you want for the column headings across the top. In each of these steps, watch the sample to see how your selections are being laid out.

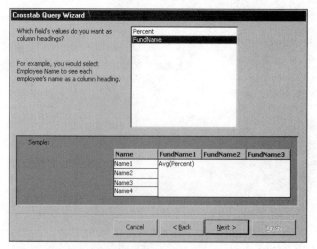

Figure Q-7   Choose the field for column headings.

5. In the fourth wizard step, in the Functions list, choose a function for the data in the central data area of the query. In this example, shown in Figure Q-8, we're summing the percent of employee investment in each fund, so click the Sum function.

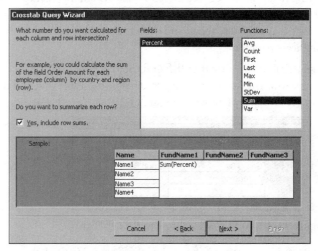

Figure Q-8   Choose the data function.

6. In the fifth wizard step, you can change the query name if you want to. Click Finish to complete the crosstab query. Figure Q-9 shows the finished example.

Name	Total Of Percent	Bahamas Portfolio	GetRichQuick Fund	Stocks'r'Us
Adrienne Willson	100		75	25
Frederick Petrof	100	35	30	35
Hans Krauser	100	40		60
Jerome Gilbert	100	34	33	33
Mary Santo	100	50	50	
Nora McGinty	100	75	25	
Ursula Andrews	100	40	40	20

Figure Q-9   A finished crosstab query.

Totals Query

Suppose you have an Orders table, and you want to know how many of each product were ordered in each state or province? You can use a query to consolidate your orders records and calculate the number of products sold in each state or province.

NOTE   *A Totals query only works on one field. In other words, you cannot consolidate data in more than one field in a single query.*

To total the entries in a field, you add two fields to the QBE grid: an identifying field, such as the StateOrProvince field in this example, and a field of numbers that can be calculated mathematically. Then you group the entries to consolidate them, and choose a consolidation *function*, or mathematical operation.

Right-click anywhere in the QBE grid, then click Totals on the shortcut menu. A new row, Total, appears in the grid below the Table row, and the default entry is Group By (shown in Figure Q-10).

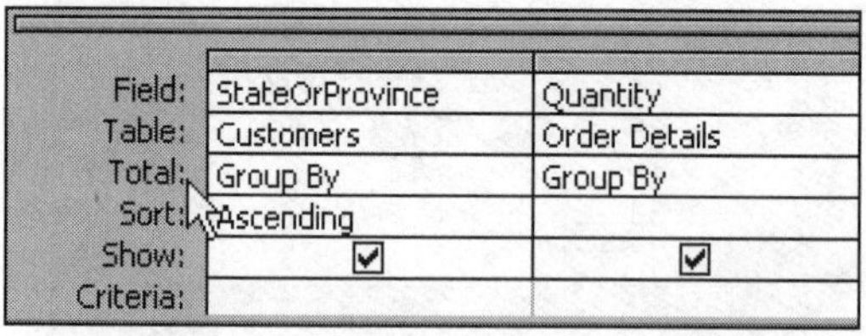

Field:	StateOrProvince	Quantity
Table:	Customers	Order Details
Total:	Group By	Group By
Sort:	Ascending	
Show:	☑	☑
Criteria:		

Figure Q-10   Add the Total row to the QBE grid.

In the field you want to total, click in the Total cell (the cell that reads Group By), and click the down arrow and select a mathematical function.

Switch to Datasheet view. Figure Q-11 shows the totals query for this example.

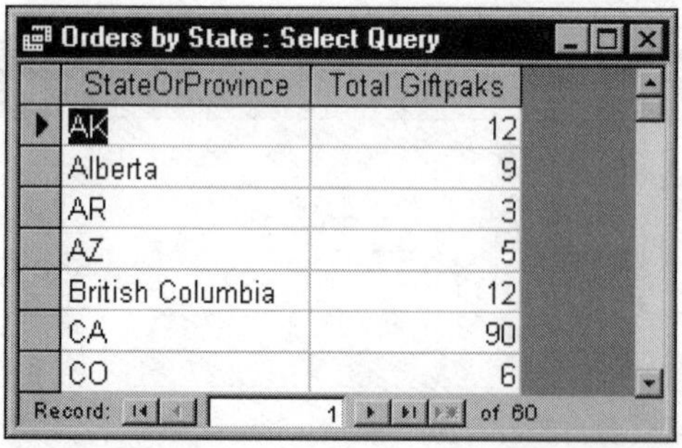

StateOrProvince	Total Giftpaks
AK	12
Alberta	9
AR	3
AZ	5
British Columbia	12
CA	90
CO	6

Record: 1 of 60

Figure Q-11   A finished totals query.

SQL Query

A SQL query is a query created by writing a SQL statement, which uses Structured Query Language to query the data. When you create any kind of query in the Access QBE grid, Access writes the SQL statement in the background. To see the SQL statement for a query, open the query, then click the arrow on the View button and choose SQL View.

Parameter Query

A parameter query is a query that asks for user-entered parameters—criteria—to determine which records to display.

You can turn an existing query into a parameter query that asks you for the records you want each time it opens. Instead of entering a specific criterion in a field's Criteria cell, you enter a user-friendly question or phrase enclosed in square brackets. To create a parameter query:

1. Open the query in Design view. In the Criteria cell for the field, type a question or phrase that asks for user input, enclosed in square brackets. For example, to create a parameter query that looks for records from a specific state in a Customers table, you can create the parameter [**What state do you want?**] in the State field. An example is shown in Figure Q-12. Be sure you type the square brackets. Every time you run the query, a dialog box will ask you which state you want and will use your entry as a query criteria.

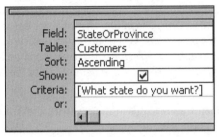

Figure Q-12   For a parameter, use any question or phrase that will make sense to a user.

TIP   *Drag the QBE grid column border to the right if you need to make the column wider.*

2. Save the query and switch to Datasheet view. The Enter Parameter Value dialog box appears with the question you typed, as shown in Figure Q-13.

Figure Q-13   What a user enters in the Enter Parameter Value dialog box is entered as the field criteria for the query.

TIP   *If your parameter doesn't work, be sure you typed square brackets around the parameter phrase.*

119

3. Type a field entry in the Enter Parameter Value dialog box and click OK. The query runs and returns all the records meeting the criterion you entered.

To remove the query parameters, delete the bracketed criterion from the query's QBE grid.

NOTE   *When you run a parameter query, you must enter the precise spelling of the entry you're looking for, but letter case doesn't matter unless you're querying a linked table.*

Append Query to Add Records

An append query is an action query. If you have a table full of duplicate records (which you may sometimes have after running a Make-Table query), or you need to append a set of records to an existing table, an append query accomplishes the task efficiently.

NOTE   *The key to eliminating duplicate records is, literally, a key—you create a new table that has the same structure as the table with the duplicate records, and in the new table you set the identifying fields as a primary key. When you run an Append query to add the records to the new table, the new table will only accept a single copy of each duplicated record, as determined by the primary key fields.*

An append query appends the records in a query to a table. You start with a query that contains all the records you want to append, and make it into an append query. To create and run an Append query:

1. Open the starting query in Design view, and choose the Query→Append Query command. In the Append dialog box, select the table name to which you want to append the query records, and click OK.

2. On the toolbar, click the Run button (it looks like an exclamation point). In the two warning messages that appear, click Yes. Close the starting query, but don't save it.

TIP   *If you save the query, it remains an Append query and appends the records to the table every time you open it—which can lead to a lot of inadvertent duplication of records in the table.*

3. Open the table to which you appended the query records. All the queried records are there.

Delete Query to Delete Records

A delete query is an action query that deletes records from a table—specifically, records you choose using a query. In a small database, deleting records might be easier by sorting, filtering, and deleting the specific records from the table manually. But if you have a table with 63,000 records, a delete query can save you time and effort.

CAUTION   *Be careful with delete queries—you can lose a lot of data, irretrievably and very quickly.*

To create and run a Delete query:

1. Create a query that shows the records you want to delete. Check your query in Datasheet view to be sure you're deleting the right records, and then return to Design view.

2. Choose the Query→Delete Query command, and then click the Run button on the Access toolbar. In the warning message, click Yes, and then close the query without saving it.

3. Open the table on which you ran the query, and use filters or sorts to look for the records you deleted (they should be gone).

NOTE   *You can easily use a delete query to delete a specific subset of records from a single table, but if you want to delete records from multiple tables in a one-to-many relationship, and referential integrity is enforced, you must have cascading deletes enabled, and you'll have to run the query twice, the first time to delete records from the primary table and the second time to delete records in the related tables.*

Make Table Query to Make a New Table

A make-table query is an action query. Sometimes you'll decide that a query's dynaset should be a new table, rather than a query. This can happen if you're creating a complex query that uses the records from other queries, or a report that's based on a query full of calculated fields—when the data gets really complex, making queried data into a new table can help you get the results you want more easily. Or, if someone asks you to export and send data that you derive using a query, you'll want to make that data into a separate table.

To make a query into a table:

1. Open (or create) the query in Design view.

2. Choose the Query→Make-Table Query command.

3. In the Make Table dialog box, name the new table, and click OK.

4. On the toolbar, click the Run button (it looks like an exclamation point).

5. In the confirmation message that appears, click Yes. Close the starting query.

   If asked to save changes, click Yes if you want to use this query to make new tables on a regular basis (it will be saved as a Make-Table Query and will make a new table every time you open it). Click No if you don't want to save the make-table query.

TIP   *If you save a query as an action query and want to change it back into a non-action query, open the query in Design view, choose the Query→Select Query command, and save the query.*

The new table you made is added to the Tables group in the database window.

Update Query to Update Records

An update query is an action query that makes identical edits to many records at once. For example, if you have a customers list that's missing the postal code entries for all customers in a particular city, you can query for those records and update the postal code for all of them at the same time.

TIP   *Sometimes an update query is better than a search-and-replace operation, because search-and-replace changes every identical entry, but an update query only changes the entries in the specific records you query.*

To create and run an update query:

1. Create a query that shows all the records in which you need to make an identical edit in a field. Check the query in Datasheet view, then return to Design view.

2. Choose the Query→Update Query command. The query window changes to an Update Query window, and an Update To row is added to the QBE grid.

3. In the field you need to edit, in the Update To cell, type the new entry. Type only the characters—Access will add the quote marks when you press Enter.

4. On the toolbar, click the Run button (it looks like an exclamation point). In the warning message, click Yes, and close the update query without saving it.

All the records are updated with the edited entry, which you can see if you open the table.

Query By Example (QBE)

Query By Example, or QBE, is a technique for creating queries by dragging and dropping fields from tables into a grid in the query Design view window. The grid is called the QBE grid.

When you use the QBE grid to create a query, Access converts your QBE layout into a SQL statement that actually runs the query. To see the SQL statement that Access created for a query: open the query, click the arrow on the View button, and choose SQL View. The SQL statement appears in the query window.

Query Calculations see Calculated Field

Query Criteria

Query criteria are used to filter records in a query. They are entered in the Criteria row in a query's QBE grid.

SEE ALSO *Criteria, Criteria Operators*

Record Selectors

In a table or query, this is the gray box at the left side of each record in a Datasheet view; you click the record selector to select the entire record.

In a form, the record selector is the vertical gray bar on the left side of the form. You can show or hide the record selector, because it's a form formatting option. This is important if you create a switchboard form, because it doesn't show records and is cluttered by extra elements like record selectors. To show or hide the record selector in a form: open the form in Design view, right-click the gray box in the upper-left corner of the form, and click Properties. On the Format tab, in the Record Selectors property box, choose Yes or No.

Record Source

Reports and forms get the data they display from a record source, which is a table or a query. If you want to change the records displayed in a form or report to show records from a different source, all you have to do is change the Record Source property.

To change the record source for a form or report: Open the object in Design view, right-click the gray box in the upper-left corner of the object, and click Properties. On the Data tab, click in the Record Source box, and choose a different table or query from the list.

If the record source for the object is a query and you only want to change the query, click the Build button (the button with three dots) next to the Record Source box to open the query window. Make your changes, click the Save button, and close the query window.

Records

Records are a set of information that belongs together, such as a customer's name and address information, or details about a product. All records are stored in tables, and each record appears as a row in a table.

Adding Records

To add a record to a table in Datasheet view, start a new record at the bottom of the table, and enter the data for the record. To add a record using a form, start a new record at the end of the existing records in the form.

To start a new record in a table or a form, you can either click the New Record button in the navigation area, or click in the last field in the last existing record and then press the Tab key.

Editing Records

To edit an existing record, whether in a table, query, or form, move the insertion point into the field you want to edit. To replace the existing entry, select the entire entry and type or select a new entry; to change a few characters, select the characters you want to change, and delete or replace them.

Saving Records

Records don't need to be saved apart from entering the data. When you enter data in a record and then move the insertion point out of the record, either to a new record or to a different existing record, any data you added or changed is automatically saved.

While you are adding or editing data in a record, a pencil symbol appears in the record selector, as shown in Figure R-1. While the pencil symbol is displayed, the changes to the record aren't saved. When you move to a different record, the record you changed is saved and the pencil symbol disappears.

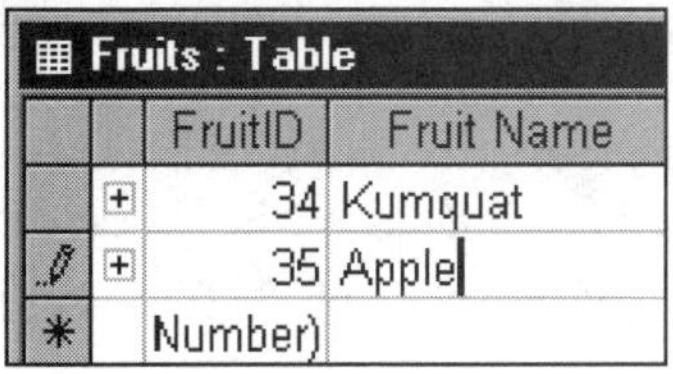

Figure R-1 The pencil symbol shows that the record isn't saved yet.

Undoing Saved Records

What if you've changed a record, it's been saved, and you decide you don't want the changes you made? If it's the most recent record you edited, you can undo your changes by choosing the Edit→Undo Saved Record command, or by clicking the Undo button on the toolbar. All the changes you made to that record are undone.

Moving Between Records

You can move from record to record in a table, query, or form by using the navigation area at the bottom of the object.

SEE ALSO *Deleting, Filters, Navigation Area, Sorting*

Redo see Undoing Mistakes

Referential Integrity

Referential integrity is a system Access uses to help enforce the accuracy of your data as time goes on. You can turn it on or off when you create or edit a table relationship. If you enforce referential integrity, Access can carry out these procedures:

- **Enforce Referential Integrity** If you mark the Enforce Referential Integrity check box without marking either of the subsidiary check boxes, you won't be allowed to change the value of a primary key in the "one" table because all the related records in the "many" table would be unmatched; and you won't be allowed to delete a record in the "one" table because all the related records in the "many" table would be orphaned. This ensures the ongoing integrity of your data, but also imposes limitations that you may not want in your tables.

- **Cascade Update Related Fields** If you mark this check box and you change a value in a primary key field in the primary table (the "one" table), Access updates the values in all the related records in the related table (the "many" table) so the relationship stays intact.

• **Cascade Delete Related Records** If you mark this check box and you delete a record in the primary table (the "one" table), Access deletes all the related records in the related table (the "many" table) instead of leaving them orphaned. Be very cautious about using the Cascade Delete Related Records option, because you can lose a lot of historical data that you didn't intend to lose.

To turn referential integrity on or off in an existing relationship: open the Relationships window and show the two related tables. Right-click the join line between them, and click Edit Relationship. In the Edit Relationships dialog box, shown in Figure R-2, mark or clear the Enforce Referential Integrity check box.

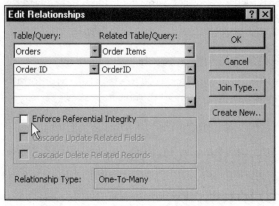

Figure R-2   Turn referential integrity on or off in the Edit Relationships dialog box.

SEE ALSO *Cascade Deletes and Updates, Relationships*

Related Table

A related table is the table on the "many" side of a one-to-many relationship.

SEE ALSO *Relationships*

Relationship Lines

Relationship lines are the lines that connect two related tables to each other when they're both displayed in a query or in the Relationships window. They're also called *join lines.*

SEE ALSO *Joins, Relationships*

Relationships

A relationship, or *join*, connects two tables, which allows you to use a query to look up and display related data that's in different tables (that's why Access is called a *relational* database). There are three types of table relationships: *one-to-one*, *one-to-many*, and *many-to-many*.

When two tables are joined, the specific fields that are joined must have matching data types. (In other words, you cannot join a text field in one table to a number field in another table, even if the entries in the two fields are identical.) The Field Size properties of the two joined fields must also match. If you're consistent about choosing data types and Field Sizes when you create tables, you will seldom run into a problem with this. To view, create, or delete table relationships, you open the Relationships window.

To open the Relationships window: close any open database objects, and click the Relationships button on the Access toolbar (or choose the Tools→Relationships command). The Relationships window appears (shown in Figure R-3). It may or may not have any tables in it, depending on whether the layout was saved the last time it was opened.

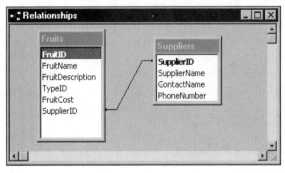

Figure R-3   The Relationships window with two related tables shown.

In the Relationships window, each table is a rectangle with the table's name in the title bar and a list of field names. If the table has a primary key field, that field name is bold. The related fields in each table are connected by a *join line*. If you can't see all the field names for a table, drag the bottom border of the table rectangle to make it longer.

To display tables in the Relationships window: right-click in a blank area of the Relationships window and click Show Table. In the Show Tables dialog box, click the table name and click Add. When you've added the tables you want to work with, click Close.

To create a relationship between two tables: click the field name in one table to select it, then drag the selected field name to the other table and drop it on the related field name.

NOTE   *The field names don't have to match, but the data types and field sizes must match. If you try to create a join and Access refuses, open each table in Design view and make sure the fields you're joining are compatible. To open a table in Design view from within the Relationships window, right-click the table and click Table Design. Then make any changes and save and close the table to return to the Relationships window.*

After you drop the one field name on the other, the Edit Relationships dialog box appears. The dialog box shows the names of the fields that you've joined, and at the bottom of the dialog box Access tells you what type of relationship this join will create (if it doesn't read one-to-one or one-to-many, you may have a problem with the relationship). Click the Create button to complete the relationship.

To delete a relationship: right-click the join line and click Delete.

One-to-One Relationship

One-to-one relationships, in which each record in one table has only one matching record in the related table, are uncommon because one-to-one data are usually kept in a single table. One reason you might want to use a one-to-one relationship between two tables is to record publicly available information about employees (such as name, department, and supervisor) in one table and private employee information (such as address, home phone, and salary) in another, less-accessible table.

One-to-Many Relationship

One-to-many relationships are the most common. In a one-to-many relationship, the table on the "one" side of the relationship is called the *primary* table. The table on the "many" side is called the *related* table.

Many-to-Many Relationship

Many-to-many relationships are also quite common. In this type of relationship, each of the tables can have many related entries in the other table.

SEE ALSO   *Junction Table*

Relationships Window

The Relationships window is where you create, edit, and delete table relationships. To open the Relationships window: close any open database objects, and click the Relationships button on the Access toolbar (or choose the Tools→Relationships command).

Showing Tables

You can show a specific table in the Relationships window, and show all the tables that are related to it, and show all the table relationships in the database.

To show specific tables in the Relationships window: right-click in the Relationships window, and click Show Table. In the Show Table dialog box (shown in Figure R-4), click the name of the table you want to show, and click the Add button. When you finish adding the tables you want, click the Close button. When you add a table that's related to a displayed table, the join line between them appears automatically.

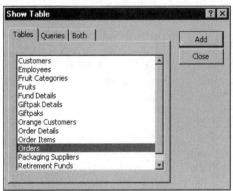

Figure R-4   Adding tables to the Relationships window with the Show Table dialog box.

To show all the tables that are directly related to a displayed table: right-click the table's title bar and click Show Direct.

To show all the related tables in the database: clear the Relationships window, then right-click the Relationships window and click Show All. Unrelated tables won't appear in the window—just those tables with relationships.

Hiding Tables

If there's a table in the Relationships window that you don't need to work with, you can remove it from the Relationships window by hiding it. To hide a table: right-click the title bar of the table rectangle, and click Hide Table.

Clearing the Relationships Window

To clear the Relationships window, click the Clear Layout button on the toolbar. Clearing the Relationships window doesn't affect the relationships, but it clears the layout of the window.

Saving the Window Layout

To save the layout of the Relationships window (the displayed tables and relationships), close the Relationships window, and when you're asked if you want to save changes, click Yes. Next time you open the Relationships window, it will open with the same layout displayed.

Report

A report is a database object that presents data in an organized, easy-to-read, printable format. The quickest way to create a report is to create an AutoReport, but AutoReports are often not very good. The easiest way to create a really good report is to use the Report Wizard. You can also create a parameter report which, like a parameter query, asks for user input before it opens.

Creating an AutoReport

To create a quick AutoReport: in the database window, select the name of the table or query for which you want a report. On the toolbar, click the arrow on the New Object button, and click AutoReport.

You can create a better-looking AutoReport with a few more steps: in the database window, select the name of the table or query for which you want a report. On the toolbar, click the arrow on the New Object button, and click Report. In the New Report dialog box, double-click either AutoReport: Columnar or AutoReport: Tabular.

Creating a Report with the Report Wizard

The Report Wizard creates a new report with your participation in parts of the layout and design process, which gives you a jump on the customization of the report. To create a report with the Report Wizard:

1. In the database window, in the Reports group, double-click Create Report By Using Wizard.
2. In the first wizard step, shown in Figure R-5, select the table(s) or query where you have the data for the report. This is easier if you've first created a single query that contains all the data you want in the report.

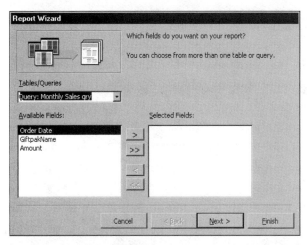

Figure R-5   Select the table or query that holds the data for the report.

3. In the Available Fields list, double-click each field you want to include in the report; or, click the double-right-arrow button to send all the fields to the Selected Fields list. Then click Next.

4. In the next wizard step, shown in Figure R-6, you can select grouping levels if you want them. When data is grouped, it's organized in a more logical manner for readers. In the list of field names, double-click each field name by which you want to group, in the order in which you want them grouped. Each group field name appears in blue in the preview window on the right side of the wizard.

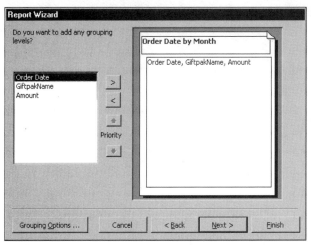

Figure R-6   Select grouping levels for the report.

5. Click Next. In this step, shown in Figure R-7, you can choose to sort the data details, and you can choose to summarize the data. To sort a field, select the field name in the uppermost sort field box, and then set the sort order. To switch the sort order, click the sort order button.

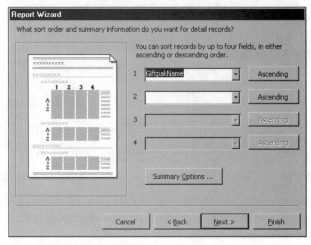

Figure R-7   Sort the data.

6. To summarize grouped data, click the Summary Options button below the sort field boxes. In the report's Summary Options dialog box, shown in Figure R-8, the fields that have calculable data are listed, and you can choose a summary function for each field you want calculated. The Details And Summary option lets the report show both details and a summarized figure for each group of data.

TIP   *If these options get confusing, the best way to figure out what you want is to create the report several times, with different options each time, and compare the results.*

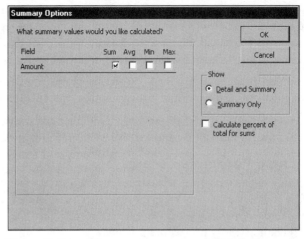

Figure R-8   Select summary options and functions.

7. Click OK to close the Summary Options dialog box, and then click Next to open the next wizard step, shown in Figure R-9. This step asks how you want the data laid out on the page. Stepped is most common, but you can click the others and see a generic preview of the selected layout. Also, if your report data has more than five or six fields, you might want to choose the Landscape option under Orientation, so that all the fields will fit on the same page more easily.

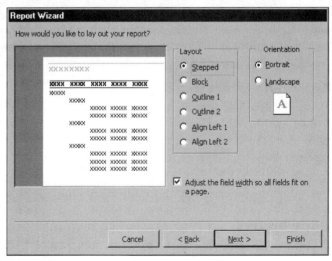

Figure R-9   Select a data layout.

8. Click Next, and choose a Style for your fonts and colors and separation lines. You can change all these things later when you customize the report, but to save yourself time and effort, start by choosing a style that's close to what you want. Click different style names to see a preview of the style.

9. Click Next. In the last wizard step, you can change the report name (usually a good idea), and click Finish to open the new report in Print Preview.

A report created by the Report Wizard is saved with the name you gave in the last wizard step, so you don't need to save it again unless you customize it.

Creating a Parameter Report

To turn an existing report into a parameter report, open the report in Design view. Right-click the gray box in the upper-left corner of the report, and click Properties. On the Data tab, click in the Record Source box, and click the Build button (the button with three dots).

The query window for the report's underlying query opens. In the Criteria row for the field in which you want user-entered criteria, type a phrase or question that asks for user input, and be sure you encase the phrase or question in square brackets. Then save and close the query window.

SEE ALSO *Queries*

Modifying a Report

You can modify a report any number of ways—by moving, resizing, or formatting controls, changing colors, adding graphic elements, removing details, and so forth. To modify a report: open the report in Design view and make your changes. Switch to Preview to check the changes, and then save the report.

Correcting Errors in a Report

If data in a report is in error, the problem is most likely not in the report, but in the underlying table where the data is stored. Close the report, open the table where the data is stored, and correct the data. When you open the report, it displays the corrected data.

TIP   *If a number appears to be truncated in the report, you may need to switch to Design view and lengthen the number's text box.*

Page Breaks

Suppose you create a report that starts a new grouped month's data at the end of the previous month's data, which is usually in the middle of the page—that means the new month group is broken over two pages. Your report may be more readable if each month begins on a new page in the report.

To change where pages break: switch the report to Design view. Right-click anywhere in the report and click Properties to open the properties sheet, then click in the area for which you want to change properties (the properties sheet shows the properties for whatever part of the report you click). As an example, you may want pages to break just before each month's group header, so each month group will begin on a new page—to do this, you click in the grouped field's Header area.

In the properties sheet (shown in Figure R-10), on the Format tab, in the Force New Page box, click the arrow and select Before Section.

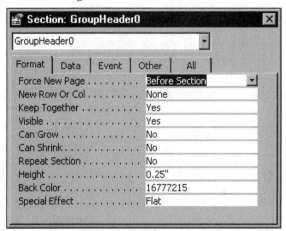

Figure R-10 Setting page breaks before each new group header.

After the page break is set, close the properties sheet and save the report.

Report Footer

A report footer contains text and/or graphics that appear at the very end of a report. Report footers often contain summaries and grand totals. You can display or hide a report footer section by opening the report in Design view and choosing the View→Report Header/Footer command.

Report Header

A report header contains text and/or graphics that appear at the very beginning of a report. Report headers often contain the report title and a company logo. You can display or hide a report header section by opening the report in Design view and choosing the View→Report Header/Footer command.

Report Preview

A report preview is the print preview you see when you open a report in Preview. The Preview view shows what the printed report will look like. To open a report in Preview: in the database window, in the Reports groups, click the name of the report and click the Preview button on the database window toolbar.

Report Snapshot

A report snapshot is a file that contains an accurate copy of each page in a report (the pages are not interactive, but they are printable). It can be viewed in the Snapshot Viewer, a standalone Microsoft Office program that's installed by Access the first time you create a snapshot. To create a report snapshot:

1. In the database window, in the Reports group, select the report name (but don't open it).

2. Choose the File→Export command.

3. In the Export dialog box, in the Save As Type box, click Snapshot Format. Navigate to the folder where you want to save the file (the snapshot file is separate from your database), type a filename in the File Name box, and click Export. If you leave the Autostart check box marked, the snapshot will be displayed in the Snapshot Viewer as soon as the file is saved.

If you send a snapshot file to a colleague, either over your network or attached to an e-mail message, your colleague can open the report by double-clicking it. If they have Office 2000 or later installed on their computer, the Snapshot Viewer will be installed from their Office software automatically.

Requerying a Query

Requerying, or running a query again, updates a query dynaset with any new records that were added since the query was opened. To run a requery: with the query open in Datasheet view, press the F9 key.

Resizing

You can resize nearly everything in database objects and windows, including column widths, row heights, control sizes, form and report background grids, windows, and text in controls and labels.

Column Widths

To resize column widths in Datasheet view, position the mouse pointer over the right border of the column header of the column you want to resize. When the mouse pointer becomes a two-headed arrow, drag to a new width. You can also double-click the column header border to make the column "best-fit" the widest entry.

Row Heights

To resize row heights in Datasheet view, position the mouse pointer over the bottom border of any row selector. When the mouse pointer becomes a two-headed arrow, drag to a new height. All the rows in an object's Datasheet view are the same height, so all will be resized to the height of the row you change.

Controls

To resize a control in a form or report, click the control to select it, and then drag one of the handles on the control's perimeter to change the size or shape. Some controls, such as check boxes and option buttons, cannot be resized.

SEE ALSO *Controls*

Form and Report Grids/Backgrounds

A form is most usable when the background is sized to fit the controls comfortably, and a report may print extra blank pages if the report's background is too large.

To change the size or shape of the grid background in a form or report, switch to Design view and position the mouse pointer over the right-side or bottom edge of the background. When the mouse pointer becomes a two-headed arrow, drag to a new size or shape. You can also drag the lower-right corner of a form or report background by positioning the mouse pointer over the lower-right corner of the background. When the mouse pointer becomes a four-headed arrow, drag to a new size or shape.

TIP　　　*You can turn the grid dots on the background on or off by choosing the View→Grid command.*

Text

You can resize the text in table and query datasheets and in controls and labels on forms and reports.

To resize the text in any Datasheet view: open the object in Datasheet view and choose the Format→Font command. In the Font dialog box, select or type a new size. The entire datasheet will be reformatted with the new font size. You cannot resize or format individual characters in a datasheet.

To resize the text in individual controls and labels: in the object's Design view, select the control or controls in which you want to resize text, and then select or type a new size in the Font Size box on the Formatting toolbar.

Resizing Form Windows to Fit

When you modify a form in Design view, you may find it easier to work in an enlarged form window; but when you switch to Form view, the window remains at the larger size. To force the window to fit the form, make sure the window isn't maximized (if it is, you'll need to restore it), and choose the Window→Size To Fit Form command.

NOTE   *When you close a form and reopen it, the window will automatically be sized to fit the form.*

Rows see Records

Saving

Saving data and database objects is simple, and Access won't let you close any changed object without asking you whether you want to save it or not. If you click Yes, the object is saved with any changes you made; if you click No, the object is closed without any of the changes you made since it was last saved.

Saving Data

Data is saved automatically as you enter it—you don't need to do anything extra to save it.

Saving a Backup Copy of Data

It's always wise to save a backup copy of your data, which will all be in the database tables. To back up a database table, you export it to another file (a file from which you can easily re-import if you need to).

You can export a table most easily to a backup Access database, in which case both the export and the re-import are quick and simple. Create a new, blank database file (don't use the wizard—you don't need any tables), name it "Backup" or something equally sensible, and export your tables to that database. Each time you export to backup, you'll replace the existing backup table with the new copy.

You can also back up tables to Excel files or any other file type in the Save As Type list in the Export dialog box.

TIP   *If you're not exporting to an Access or Excel file, run the export and then attempt to re-import the backup file to a new table in your database. Some file types, such as Text files, can be difficult to re-import and you should avoid them.*

Saving Database Files

You save a database file when you first create it and give it a name. After that, you save objects in the database file, but you don't need to save the database file itself.

Saving Database Objects

Whenever you create a new database object, you'll be asked to give it a name and it will be saved. Each time you make a change to a database object, such as changing a table field property or a report layout, you'll be asked if you want to save your changes when you close the object. If you want to save changes to any object before you close it, click the Save button on the Access toolbar.

SEE ALSO   *Exporting Data*

Select Query see Queries

Selected Record Box see Navigation Area

Selecting Objects

To select a database object, such as a form or report, open the object group in the database window and click the object's name.

To select a control in the Design view of a form or report, click the control. To select several adjacent controls, drag with the mouse to "lasso" the controls you want to select. Be sure the lasso touches each control you want—the controls do not have to be completely surrounded by the lasso.

To select several non-adjacent controls, click the first to select it, then hold down the Shift key while you click the others you want to select.

Sending Data to Excel see Exporting Data

Show Box in Query Fields

In a query's Design view, in the QBE grid, each field column has a check box (shown in Figure S-1). The check box is the Show box. If it's marked, the field data is displayed in the query; if it's cleared, the field data is used in the query (for example, to filter or sort) but not displayed in the query's Datasheet view.

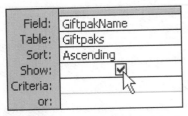

Figure S-1   The check box in the field column is the Show box.

Simple Query see Query

Sizing see Resizing

Snapshots see Report Snapshot

Sorting

Sorting is an efficient method of organizing data, and Access makes it easy to sort data in any of your tables, queries, forms, and reports. You can sort table and query datasheets by a specific field to make the data easier to use for different purposes, and you can sort data in a form so you can scroll through individual records more efficiently.

When you close an object after a sort operation, Access asks if you want to save changes to the design of the object. If you click Yes, the object (table, query, or form) will be saved with the new sort order and will re-open with that sort order in place. If you click No, the object is closed with its original sort order.

Sorting Records by a Single Field

Single-field sorting is the most common and quickest way to sort records. To sort records in a datasheet by a single field: click any cell in the field by which you want to sort. On the toolbar, click the Sort Ascending or Sort Descending button.

NOTE   *In an ascending sort, a text field is sorted in alphabetical order (A–Z), and a numeric field is sorted in numerical order (1-10). In a descending sort, a text field is sorted in alphabetical order (Z-A), and a numeric field is sorted in numerical order (10-1).*

Sorting Records by Multiple Fields

Suppose you want to see a datasheet sorted by one field within another field (for example, in a Customers table, you might want to sort the list by state, and then by last name within each state). This is called a multiple-key sort, and you do it in the Advanced Filter/Sort dialog box. To perform a multiple-key sort:

1. Open the table or query you want to sort, and choose the Records→Filter→Advanced Filter/Sort command. The Filter window opens, as shown in Figure S-2. The top half of the window is called the Table pane, and the rectangle represents the table and all of its fields.

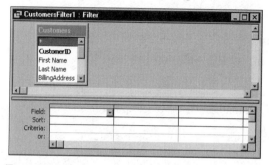

Figure S-2   The Filter window for multiple-key sorts.

TIP   *If you can't see all the field names in the table, drag the bottom of the table rectangle longer. If you need more room for the longer table rectangle, point to the two narrow bars that separate the upper and lower panes, and when the pointer becomes a two-headed arrow, drag to make the upper pane longer.*

The lower half of the window is called the filter/sort grid. You build a multiple-key sort by adding each sort field to the grid and setting a sort order in the field's Sort row.

Access sorts the fields in the grid from left to right. If, for example, you want to sort a Customers table by state and then by last name within each state, you place the state field on the left and the last name field to its right.

NOTE   *You want to clear all previous sorts and filters from the Filter window. If there's already a field name in the filter/sort grid (from a previous sort or filter), point to the gray bar at the top of the field name in the grid. When the mouse pointer becomes a down arrow, click the gray bar to select the field, then press Delete.*

2. In the Table pane, in the table rectangle, double-click the first field in your multiple-key sort to add it to the filter grid.

3. In the Table pane, double-click the next field in your multiple-key sort to add it to the filter grid.

4. Click in the Sort row under the each field, click the arrow, and click a sort order (Ascending or Descending). Figure S-3 shows the Filter window set up to sort a Customers table by StateOrProvince and then by LastName.

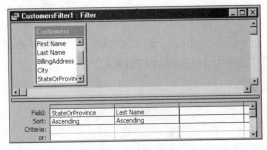

Figure S-3 A multiple-key sort set up to run.

5. Choose the Filter→Apply Filter/Sort command.

TIP   *You can also click the Apply Filter toolbar button to apply the advanced sort. If you don't see the toolbar, right-click the menu bar and choose Filter/Sort to display the Filter/Sort toolbar.*

Switch to Datasheet view to see the sorted datasheet. When you close the datasheet, you'll be asked if you want to save changes. Click No to remove the sort, or Yes to preserve the new sort order in the datasheet.

TIP   *To save a table with a specific sort order, open the table, perform the sort you want, and then save the table; the table will retain whatever sort order you save it with.*

Sorting a Form

To sort the records in a form, click in the field by which you want to sort, and click the Sort Ascending or Sort Descending button on the Access toolbar.

Sorting a Report

If you've selected a sort order in the Report Wizard when building a report, you'll find the report is properly sorted when it's finished. But you can change the sort order of any field in the report.

To change the sort order for a report: open the report in Design view, and choose the View→Sorting And Grouping command. The Sorting And Grouping dialog box appears, shown in Figure S-4.

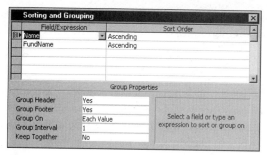

Figure S-4   Setting a different sort order in a report.

In the Sorting And Grouping dialog box, the fields on which the report data is grouped and sorted are listed in the Field/Expression column. The icon in the gray row selector, shown next to the EmployeeID field in Figure S-4, indicates that the report data is grouped by that field. All the field names listed in the Field/Expression column have sort orders applied.

To change a field's sort order, click in the field's Sort Order cell and select the other sort order. To add a new field for sorting, click in an empty cell in the Field/Expression column, select the field name, and then select a sort order for the field in the Sort Order column.

Switch to Preview to see the results of your changes before you save the report. If you don't like the changes, you can undo the changes you made in the Sorting And Grouping dialog box, or close the report without saving it.

Removing a Sort from a Table, Query, or Form

To remove a sort from a table, query, or form: you can choose the Records→Remove Filter/Sort command, or close the object without saving it.

Removing a Sort from a Report

To remove a sort order from a report, open the report in Design view. Choose the View→Sorting And Grouping command. In the Sorting And Grouping dialog box, click the row selector for the field you want to remove from sorting, and press Delete.

Speech Recognition

Office XP supports speech recognition, which means that you can use speech recognition with any of the programs that make up Office XP including Access 2002. However, a database cannot be accurately sorted, filtered, or queried if words are not spelled consistently—and speech recognition can inadvertently enter incorrect words, which can make your database work poorly unless you catch those mistakes. For this reason, you almost certainly will not use speech recognition with Access (even though you may choose to use speech recognition with other programs such as Word 2002).

Spelling

You can use the Tools→Spelling command to check spelling in your tables, forms and queries. When you choose the command, Access displays the Spelling dialog box (shown in Figure S-5). Access identifies words it doesn't recognize in the Not In Dictionary box. In the Suggestions box, Access suggests alternatives. To make a suggested fix, double-click it. To ignore the error, click the Ignore button. To add the word to a custom dictionary because it is correctly spelled and you will use it again and again in your documents, click the Add To Dictionary button.

NOTE   *Any changes the Spelling Checker makes are made in the underlying table, even if you make the changes in a form or query.*

Because database data tends to contain many names and other words that aren't likely to be in the dictionary, you can have Access skip specific fields that are likely to have lots of unrecognized words. Click the Ignore '*field name*' Field button, and the Spelling Checker moves on to the next field.

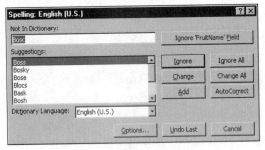

Figure S-5   The Spelling dialog box.

The Options button on the Spelling And Grammar box displays the Spelling dialog box. (You can also get to this tab of options by choosing the Tools→Options command and clicking the Spelling tab.)

- Use the Dictionary Language box to select the dictionary you want to use for checking the spelling.

- Select the dictionary that Access should add new words to using the Add Words To box.

- Check the Suggest From Main Dictionary Only box to tell Access to only use the main Access dictionary for spell checking.

- Check the Ignore Words In UPPERCASE box to tell Access it should ignore words that use all uppercase letters (presumably because these are acronyms or abbreviations that won't be in the dictionary).

- Check the Ignore Words With Numbers to tell Access that it should ignore words that combine letters and numbers (presumably because you're using things like product names or serial numbers that won't be in the dictionary).

- Check the Ignore Internet And File Addresses box to tell Access it should ignore Internet URLs and file pathnames when it checks spelling.

- The AutoCorrect Options button opens the AutoCorrect dialog box, where you can create AutoCorrect entries.

SEE ALSO   *AutoCorrect*

SQL Server

SQL Server (SQL is pronounced "sequel") is any database management system that can respond to queries that are written in the SQL (Structured Query Language) language. Two popular server systems in use are Microsoft SQL Server and Sybase SQL Server. When the data load in a database such as Access becomes extremely large, it's sensible to move the data to a SQL Server for storage. The data stored in a SQL Server can be utilized by the objects in an Access project just as if it were stored in a local Access database.

SEE ALSO *Access Project*

Starting Access

You can start Access either by starting the program directly or by opening an existing Access database. To start Access directly, click the Start button, choose Programs, and then choose Microsoft Access. When you do this, Access starts and the New File task pane appears on the right.

To open an Access database—which indirectly starts Access—you can double-click an Access database file (which has an icon with a key symbol and, if you're viewing file extensions, has the extension .MDB) in the My Computer or Windows Explorer window. If you've recently used the file, you can also open it from the Documents menu by clicking the Start button, choosing Documents, and choosing the Access database you want to open. When you do this, Access starts and opens the database you selected.

NOTE   *You can also create desktop shortcuts that point to the Access program or to individual databases. When you open a shortcut, Windows starts the program or opens the database that the shortcut points to. For information on creating and using shortcuts, refer to the Windows help file.*

Startup Macro see Macros

Status Bar

The status bar is the bar at the bottom of your screen that displays information about the activity on your screen. For example, when you enter data in a table or form, whatever is entered in the table's Description column for a particular field is displayed in the status bar while the insertion point is in that field.

SEE ALSO *Tables*

Stopping Access

To stop the Access program, choose the File→Exit command or click the Access program window's Close button (in the upper-right corner).

SEE ALSO *Starting Access*

Subform Control

A subform control is the rectangular control that represents the subform when the main form is in Design view. A subform control has properties that are different and separate from the properties of the subform itself. Subforms can be *nested*, or contained one within another — you can place as many subforms as you want in a single main form, and each subform in a main form can contain a single subform of its own.

If the combination main form/subform was created by the AutoForm Wizard from two tables, it will look like the one shown in Figure S-6. You won't be able to open and format the subform control, although you can resize it in the main form's Design view.

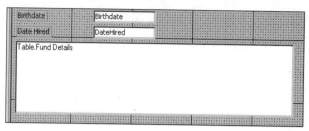

Figure S-6   This subform control was created by a wizard and can't be formatted.

SEE ALSO *Subforms*

Subforms

A subform is a form within a main form, which shows records that are related to the active record in the main form. A subform is a separate form that can be formatted if it's created as a separate form and then dropped into the main form, or if it's created by the Form Wizard from two tables. Figure S-7 shows a subform in Design view that can be formatted separately from the main form.

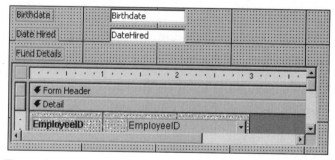

Figure S-7   This form has a subform that can be formatted separately.

To create a separate subform, create the main form and subform as two separate forms, and be sure the underlying tables are joined in a relationship. Then open the main form in Design view, and drag the name of the subform from the database window and drop it in the main form's grid. Double-click in the subform's border to open the Subform/Subreport properties sheet shown in Figure S-8. The Link Child Fields and Link Master Fields boxes should have the related fields displayed—if not, you can select the appropriate fields from the boxes.

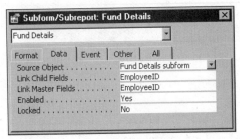

Figure S-8   The Link Child Fields and Link Master Fields boxes are where the main form/subform relationship is established.

Removing the Subform Navigation Area

A subform's navigation area is usually unnecessary and can be confusing during data entry. To remove it: open the main form/subform in Design view. Right-click the gray box in the upper-left corner of the subform control and click Properties. On the Format tab, in the Navigation Buttons property box, select No.

SUM Function see Functions

Switchboard

Most wizard-built databases have an opening switchboard like the one shown in Figure S-9. A switchboard is a form that doesn't show any records or data; instead, it has buttons that perform actions such as opening other database objects. Switchboards make a database much easier for a non-expert to use, but if you find a switchboard to be a nuisance, you can delete it without altering database function. You can also create your own switchboard for a database you create without the wizard.

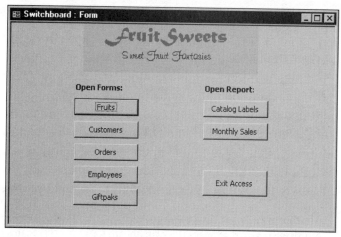

Figure S-9   A switchboard form.

To create your own switchboard: in the database window, in the Forms group, double-click Create Form In Design View. A blank form grid opens, and you can add command button controls from the toolbox to perform database actions, and labels to show information and instructions.

SEE ALSO   *Controls, Form*

Removing Unnecessary Switchboard Features

If you create your own switchboard form, you won't want the usual form features such as scrollbars, record selectors, navigation buttons, and so forth. All of these items are formatting features. To remove them (and others): open the switchboard form in Design view, right-click in the gray box in the upper-left corner of the form, and click Properties. On the Format tab, in the property boxes for each property or feature you want to remove, select No or Neither.

Setting to Open at Database Startup

A switchboard is most useful if it opens automatically when the database starts up. To set a switchboard (or any other database object) to open automatically at startup: close all open database objects. Choose the Tools→Startup command. In the Startup dialog box, shown in Figure S-10, select the name of your switchboard form in the Display Form/Page box.

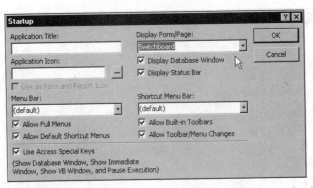

Figure S-10   Setting a switchboard form to display at database startup.

Another way to set the switchboard to open at startup is to create an AutoExec macro that opens the switchboard form. AutoExec macros always run at startup.

SEE ALSO *AutoExec Macro*

Deleting

To delete a switchboard, in the database window, in the Forms group, select the switchboard form name and press Delete.

Minimizing

If you don't want to close the switchboard form, but want it out of your way while you work, click the Minimize button in the form's upper-right corner.

Closing

To close a switchboard form, click the Close button in the form's upper-right corner.

Tab Order

Tab order is the order in which the focus moves from control to control on a form when you press the Tab key.

SEE ALSO *Forms*

Table Relationships see Relationships

Tables

A table is a collection of data with the same subject or topic. Data are stored in records (rows) and fields (columns). Tables are the core of any database because tables are where all the data is stored (all other objects just provide different ways of looking at the table data).

There are several ways to create tables in Access, and which you choose depends on where your data is and your personal preferences.

In the Tables group in the database window, you find three techniques for creating new tables. If you click the New button in the database window, the New Table dialog box opens with those three techniques and two more.

- **Datasheet View**: Choosing Datasheet View in the New Table dialog box is the same as choosing Create A Table By Entering Data in the database window. Using this technique, you build a table by entering field headings and a single row of data for the table—Access determines the data type for each field from the data you enter.

- **Design View**: Choosing Design View in the New Table dialog box is the same as choosing Create A Table In Design View in the database window. Using this technique, you create each field name, data type, and primary key yourself (no letting Access guess).

- **Table Wizard**: Choosing Table Wizard in the New Table dialog box is the same as choosing Create Table By Using Wizard in the database window. A wizard opens with a list of sample tables and fields (Business or Personal). You choose a Sample Table name, double-click Sample Field names to add them to your new table, and follow the wizard steps to finish the table.

- **Import Table**: If your data already exists in a computer file, click the New button and then double-click Import Table. You can import data from another Access database, an Excel workbook, a dBase, Paradox, or other database, a text file, or an Outlook folder. Importing data brings a copy of the data into your database.

- **Link Table**: If your data already exists in a computer file, and you want to use the data without making a separate copy of it in your database, click the New button and then double-click Link Table. If, for example, you need to use data that's maintained in an Excel worksheet in another department in your company, you can create a linked file that gives you full access to the data, and the data will always be current because the only copy is maintained by the other department.

SEE ALSO *Tables, Importing; Tables, Linking*

Creating Tables Using the Wizard

The wizard can create a table for you from a list of built-in sample tables, each with lots of sample fields and appropriate data types. All you need to do is follow the wizard steps and choose from the options you see.

To create a new table using the wizard: in the database window, in the Tables group, double-click Create Table By Using Wizard.

1. In the first Table Wizard dialog box, click the Business or Personal option (each category offers a different set of sample tables). Choose the table in the Sample Tables list that's most appropriate for your data.

2. In the Sample Fields box, shown in Figure T-1, double-click each field that you want in the new table. If you make a mistake and accidentally move a field you don't want, double-click it to return it to the Sample Fields list.

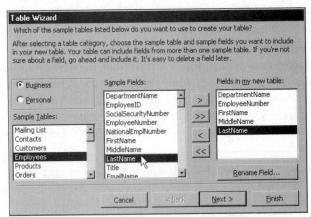

Figure T-1   Choosing fields in the Table Wizard.

NOTE   *To rename a field, select it in the Fields In My New Table list and then click the Rename Field button. In the Rename Field dialog box, type a new name and click OK. (Field names can include blank spaces and be more than one word long, but that's not a good database practice. If you ever export this table to another database program, poor names can cause someone a lot of extra work to clean up.)*

3. Click Next, and in the next step, name the table and decide if you want the wizard to choose a primary key for you.

4. Click Next. If you clicked the No, I'll Set The Primary Key option in the previous step, Access assumes that one of your fields will be the primary key field. The next wizard step asks you to select that field and choose a method of entering the primary key data. If you clicked the Yes, Set A Primary Key For Me option in the previous step, you'll skip the primary key information step and move to the next wizard step.

5. If your database already includes a table, the next wizard step asks how the table you are creating relates to the table or tables already in the database. You can let the wizard create a relationship, if there is one, or you can avoid letting the wizard create the relationship and create it yourself later.

6. Click Next. In the last Table Wizard step, choose an option and click Finish. The Modify The Table Design option switches the finished table to Design view; the Enter Data Directly Into The Table option opens the finished table in Datasheet view so you can start entering data; and the Enter Data Into The Table Using A Form That The Wizard Creates For Me option creates and opens a simple form you can use to enter data in the table.

Creating Tables in Design View

To create a new table in Design view, double-click Create Table In Design View in the database window. An empty table in Design view appears (shown in Figure T-2). This is the technique that most Access professionals use, because it provides direct, detailed control over the new table from the very start.

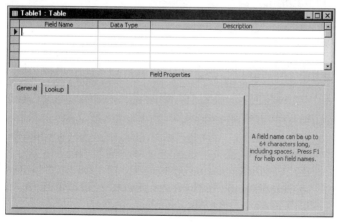

Figure T-2   An empty table in Design view.

To build the table:

1. In the Field Name column, in the first row, type a field name. Good database practice stipulates that the field name have no spaces in it (names with no spaces are always easier for any program to work with), but an easy way to use a multiple-word name is to initial-cap each word and remove the spaces, as in "ZipCode" or "LastName."

2. In the same row, click in the Data Type column, and click the down arrow that appears (as shown in Figure T-3). The data type you choose for that field limits the kind of data that can be entered in the field, which helps to keep your data accurate.

TIP   *A simple rule is this: if the field's data won't be calculated (names, zip codes, dates), choose Text. If the data will be calculated (quantities, dollars), choose Number or Currency. If the entry is extraneous notes about the record, choose Memo. If the entry is always a simple yes or no, choose Yes/No.*

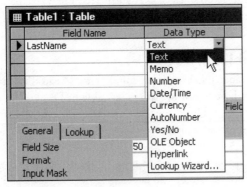

Figure T-3   Set a data type for the field.

3. In the Description column, type a description of the data that should be entered in that field. The description is optional; whatever you type here will be visible in the taskbar when someone is entering data in that field in Datasheet view of the table.

4. If you need a primary key (you won't always, but it helps you keep your data accurate), click in the field that should be the primary key, and click the Primary Key button on the toolbar. To add an ID field which is automatically numbered by Access, create the field (name it anything you like), and give it the AutoNumber data type.

5. When you're finished, click the Save button on the toolbar, give the table a name, and click OK. Then click the View button on the left end of the toolbar to switch to Datasheet view and enter data in the table.

Creating Tables by Entering Data

To create a new table in Datasheet view, double-click Create Table By Entering Data in the Tables group in the database window. A new, blank table datasheet like the one in Figure T-4 opens.

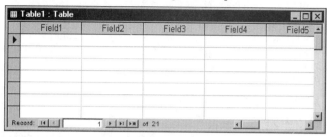

Figure T-4 A new, blank table datasheet.

To make this new, blank table datasheet into a table in your database:

1. Double-click on each field heading (the field heading is selected, as shown in Figure T-5), type a field name, and press Enter. Don't worry about the extra blank fields—they'll disappear after you save the table.

Figure T-5 Double-click a field heading to type a new field name.

2. Enter a single row of typical data for the table, as shown in Figure T-6. To enter data, click in a cell and type the data, then press Enter or Tab.

FirstName	LastName	Birthdate	Phone
Hal	Smith	1/1/55	800-555-1234

Figure T-6 Enter a single row of typical data for the table.

TIP   *If you need to rearrange your columns, click on the field heading to select the column, then drag the field heading to a different position in the headings row. If you want to rename a field heading while you're building the table, double-click it again and type a new heading. At this stage, the new table is very easy to reconfigure (you can reconfigure later, but it's easier to do it now).*

3. When you're happy with the table configuration and you've got one row of data entered, click the Save button on the Access toolbar.

4. In the Save As dialog box that appears, type a name for the table and click OK. Access asks you if you want to define a primary key now. A primary key is not needed in every table (and can make a table more cumbersome to customize), but until you know more about table customization, you might as well click Yes and let Access create a primary key in your table. The primary key field Access adds is a new field named "ID." Every time you add a new row of data, Access creates a new, unique, sequential entry in the primary key field.

You can continue entering data in the new table, or close it and enter the data later.

Modifying Tables

To modify a table, open it in Design view. You can add new fields, delete fields, rearrange fields, and change field data types and properties.

NOTE   *Once the table is full of data, it may be impossible to change a field's data type without losing all the data in that field—so choose data types carefully when you first create your fields.*

Primary Key Problems

Primary keys function to uniquely identify every record in a table. To do that, they can't allow any duplicate values or null (no entry) values to be entered in the field you designate as the primary key.

If a table already holds data and you are unable to set a field as a primary key, you may have a null or duplicate value in the field. Sort the table by that field, and locate and change the problem value; then try setting the field as the primary key again.

If you are importing or appending data to an existing table which has a primary key set, one or more records might not be allowed into the existing table because the imported values violate the primary key integrity in the existing table. One solution to this problem is to remove the conflicting field from the imported table, then import the records, and enter appropriate values for the primary key field after the import.

SEE ALSO *Data Types, Field, Field Properties, Primary Key*

Tables, Importing

If your data is already in an electronic file, such as an Excel workbook or a table in another database, there's no point in re-typing any of it. You can import the data neatly into your Access database and make any modifications you need after the table is imported. To import the data into the database:

1. In the database window, click the New button on the toolbar. In the New Table dialog box, double-click Import Table.

2. In the Import dialog box, navigate to the folder where the data is stored, and in the Files Of Type box, select the type of file in which the data is stored.

3. Double-click the name of the file you want to import. The next sequence of dialog boxes depends on what type of file you're importing.

   - If you're importing an Excel file, the Import Spreadsheet Wizard starts. Follow the steps in the wizard to import the data into a new Access table.

   - If you're importing data from an existing database such as Access, the Import Objects dialog box opens, and you can choose the table name to import (you can import any objects from another Access database). The selected objects are copied into the open database.

   - If you're importing a text file, the Import Text Wizard starts. Follow the steps in the wizard to import the data into a new Access table.

SEE ALSO *Importing Data, Text Files*

Tables, Junction see Junction Table

Tables, Linking

If the data you need is in another file or database, and needs to remain in that other file or database, it's best to link to the existing table rather than create a new copy of the data in your database. For example, if you need to use a list of customers that's maintained by the Orders department, it's not a good idea to import the list into your database, because when the customer data changes in the Orders department's list, your imported table won't be current. But if your table is linked to the Orders department's list, their current data will always be available in your database. To create a linked table:

1. In the database window, in the Tables group, click the New button on the toolbar. In the New Table dialog box, double-click Link Table.

2. In the Link dialog box, choose the file type you want to link to in the Files Of Type box, then navigate to the folder where the data is stored, and double-click the name of the file or database that you want to link to.

3. If the file is an Excel workbook, the Link Spreadsheet Wizard starts—follow the wizard steps to make sure the data is parsed and labeled correctly and give the linked table a name. If the linked table is in another Access database, the Link Tables dialog box appears—click the name of the table, and click OK. (Whatever file type you're linking to, the appropriate wizard or dialog box is fairly self-explanatory.)

Figure T-7 shows a Tables group in a database window, and in the list of tables are two linked tables (identified by the arrows to the left of the table icons).

Figure T-7   A database window with two linked tables—one linked Access table, and one linked Excel table.

Linked tables work just like tables that exist in your database, except that you won't be able to modify them in Design view (but all you need is the data in them, so that won't be a problem). From within your database, you can enter and edit data in a linked table, join it to other tables in your database for queries and reports, and create forms for entering and editing data in the linked table.

Task Pane

The task pane, the vertical pane that appears on the right side of the program window whenever you start an Office program, is a new feature in all the programs in the Office XP suite. It's a central point for many tasks and procedures. If you find that it's in your way while you work, you can close it by clicking the X box in its upper-right corner.

TIP   *You can still open existing databases with the earlier method—by choosing the File→Open command and locating the database file in the Open dialog box.*

Taskbar

The Windows taskbar displays the Start button, which you can use to display the menus you'll use to start Access or open a recently used database. The taskbar also displays other buttons to open programs and files. You can switch between open programs and files by clicking the buttons on the taskbar.

Text Box

A text box is a control that displays a value from a table field or from an expression's calculation. It's often used to enter or edit data in a field.

SEE ALSO *Controls*

Text Files

Text files are files that contain data only, no formatting. They can be simple documents such as those you can create in Windows Notepad, or they can be tables of data that are separated into columns. The columns may be *fixed-width*, meaning that each column is a specific number of characters wide, or they may be *delimited*, meaning that the column entries are separated by specific characters, usually a Tab character or a comma.

Access lets you easily import or link text files into a database. Anything you can get as a text file—such as a customer list generated by the mainframe computer—can be linked or imported into an Access database and then used.

If you use the File→Open command to open a text file from within Access, a new database and a linked table are created. If you want to link or import the text file into an existing database, open the database and use the File→Get External Data→Import or File→Get External Data→Link Tables command.

Regardless of which command you use, one of the Text File Wizards opens and helps you to link or import the text file into Access.

1. In the first dialog box that appears (Open, Import, or Link), navigate to the folder where the text file is located, and select Text Files in the Files Of Type box so that your text file is listed in the dialog box. Click the file name and then click the Open (or Import or Link) button. Access displays the first Wizard dialog box (shown in Figure T-8).

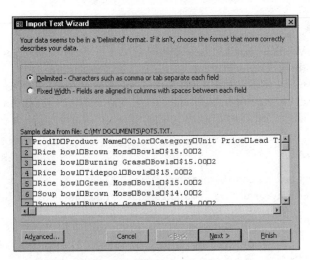

Figure T-8   The first Wizard dialog box.

2. Use the option buttons—Fixed Width or Delimited—to indicate whether the file uses a fixed-width format, in which each column is a fixed width, or uses delimiting characters. Access can usually guess correctly about which format your text file uses, so if you're not sure which option to select, accept Access's default suggestion. You'll see the results of your choice in the next dialog box.

3. Click Next. Access displays the second Wizard dialog box (see either Figure T-9 or Figure T-10). If you're importing a fixed-width file, Access displays the dialog box shown in Figure T-9. You use this dialog box to verify how Access breaks the text file into columns. You can create new break lines by clicking. You can remove an existing break line by double-clicking. You can also move an existing break line by dragging.

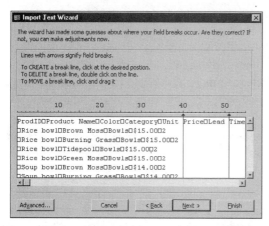

Figure T-9   The second Wizard dialog box if you're importing a fixed-width file.

If you're importing a delimited character file, Access displays the dialog box shown in Figure T-10. You use this dialog box principally to verify that Access has correctly identified the delimiter: the marked Delimiters option identifies the delimiter. You can also indicate if the text file uses a character (such as a quotation mark) to identify text. You can tell whether Access's delimiter assumptions correctly describe the text file because the preview box shows how your data look using the selected delimiter.

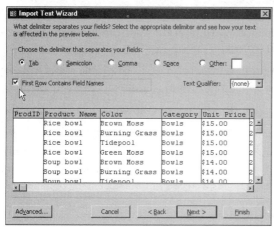

Figure T-10   The second Wizard dialog box if you're importing a delimited character file.

If the first row of data contains field names, click the First Row Contains Field Names check box.

4. After you've verified the fixed-width or delimited character assumptions of Access—and fixed any incorrect assumptions—click Next. Access displays the third Wizard dialog box. If you're importing the text file into a database, the third Wizard dialog box lets you choose whether to create a new table or import the data into an existing table. Click the option you want (and select the table name if you're importing into an existing table), and click Next.

If you're importing into an existing table, the next dialog box will be the last—go to step 7.

NOTE   *If you're importing the data into an existing table, both tables must be identical in structure, or the data won't be imported properly. Importing the data into an existing table is most efficient when the existing table was created by importing this particular text file, and then you import the same text file (with updated data) on a regular schedule to keep your Access data updated.*

If you're linking to the file, you won't see this dialog box—instead, you'll go on to step 5.

5. In the next dialog box, Access guesses about the default formatting that it should use for each field (column) of the text file you import—you should verify the formatting that's assigned to each field, because it will affect how your database functions. To change a field's format, click the column header and then check or change the entry in the Data Type box. If you don't want to import a column, click it and then click the Do Not Import Field (Skip) check box.

6. Click Next. If you're importing the text file, the wizard will ask you about adding a primary key. Choose the option you want, and click Next.

If you're linking the file, you won't be asked about a primary key—instead, you'll see the last dialog box, in step 7.

7. In the last dialog box, Access asks you what to name the table. Type the name you want in the Import To Table box or the Linked Table Name box, and click Finish. Access finishes the linking or importing process.

SEE ALSO *Primary Key, Tables*

Tiling Windows see Windows

Toolbars

A toolbar is the horizontal bar that contains toolbar buttons that you can click to carry out menu or macro commands (in Access, the toolbar changes depending on which object and view are displayed).

Identifying Toolbar Buttons

To identify a toolbar button or box, point to the tool. Excel displays a ScreenTip with the tool's name. To get a description of what a button does, choose the Help→What's This? command, and then click on the button you want explained.

Displaying and Removing Toolbars

Access displays a particular toolbar when you're working with items that toolbar supplies buttons for. For example, if you're working in a form's Design view, the Form Design toolbar appears.

You can also control when a toolbar is displayed. Choose the View→Toolbars command and then select the toolbar you want. The commands listed on the Toolbars submenu are toggle commands. Access places a check mark in front of those toolbars that are displayed. To remove a toolbar, choose the View→Toolbars command and select the displayed toolbar you want to remove.

NOTE   *You cannot display a toolbar for an item that's not open—for example, you can't display the Form Design toolbar unless there's a form open in Design view.*

Customizing a Toolbar

The Access toolbars are well-equipped for everything you need to do, but if you create a macro, you may want to add a custom toolbar button to run the macro. To add buttons to a toolbar:

1. Make sure the toolbar is currently visible. Choose the Tools→Customize command and click the Commands tab (shown in Figure T-11).

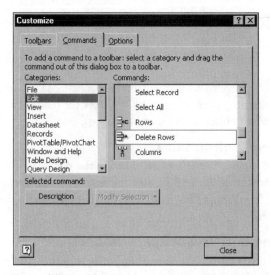

Figure T-11   The Commands tab of the Customize dialog box.

2. Select the command category from the Categories list box that includes the command you want to add to a toolbar.

3. Scroll through the Commands list box. When you see the command you want to add to the toolbar, drag it to the toolbar.

   If you're creating a new button to run a saved macro, choose the All Macros category and drag the name of the macro to the toolbar.

   While the Customize dialog box is open, you can change the image, label, ScreenTip name, and hot key for the button.

NOTE   *You can also customize a toolbar by clicking on the arrow button at the far right end of the toolbar, choosing the Add Or Remove buttons command, and then the name of the toolbar. For example, to customize the Database toolbar, click the arrow button and choose Add Or Remove Buttons and then Database. Access displays a complete list of the buttons commonly placed on the toolbar. To add a button, select it from the list.*

To remove a button from a toolbar:

1. Click on the arrow button at the far right end of the toolbar.

2. Choose the Add Or Remove buttons command, and then the name of the toolbar. For example, to customize the Database toolbar, click the arrow button, choose Add Or Remove Buttons and then Database.

3. When Access displays a complete list of the buttons commonly placed on the toolbar, select the button you want to remove. Access identifies which buttons are already on the toolbar by marking them with a check mark.

TIP   *You can remove a button very quickly by pressing the Alt key while you drag the button away from the toolbar. You can also rearrange buttons on a toolbar by pressing the Alt key while you drag buttons to new positions.*

Customizing Button Images and Names

Customizing a button image or ScreenTip name is great for making your custom buttons (such as those that you create to run a macro) more visually intuitive. To customize a button image or name, the Customize dialog box must be open (even though you won't actually use the dialog box).

Right-click a toolbar and choose Customize, then right-click the button you want to customize. Choose commands on the shortcut menu to customize the button.

- To change the ScreenTip name, enter the new name in the Name box.

- To create a hot key for the button, type an ampersand (&) in front of the letter that will be the hot key.

- To change the button image, choose Change Button Image, and then click a new image.

- To draw your own button image, choose Edit Button Image, and draw your own image by coloring the pixels in the Button Editor.

- To remove an image and show only the button name on the button, choose Text Only (Always).

- To remove label text and show only the button image on the button, choose Text Only (In Menus).

Toolbox

The Toolbox is the floating toolbar (shown in Figure T-12) that contains the buttons for creating controls in forms and reports. It appears only in Design view. If it doesn't appear when you switch a form or report to Design view, click the Toolbox button on the Design toolbar.

Figure T-12   The Controls Toolbox.

SEE ALSO *Controls*

Totals Query see Queries

Troubleshooting

You can suffer from two types of trouble when you work with Access.

The first type of trouble amounts to operational trouble working with the program—often because you're still learning how to use Access. When you experience this type of trouble—and assuming you can't get your answer from this book—use the Ask A Question box to ask a question. If you don't get the answer from the first set of help topics that the Ask A Question box suggests, try rephrasing your question using different words.

The second type of trouble stems from software problems with the Access program itself or perhaps one of the other programs running on your computer. Surprisingly, you often can solve software problems, too, if you visit Microsoft's Knowledge Base web site. The Microsoft Knowledge Base web site provides troubleshooting information about solving all sorts of software problems and bugs working with Access.

To use the Microsoft Knowledge Base web site, open your web browser and enter the following URL into the Address box:

http://search.support.microsoft.com/kb

Unbound Control

An unbound control is a control that's not bound (connected) to a specific field in a query or table. You can use an unbound control to display general information or to perform calculations on the values in other controls in a form or report.

SEE ALSO *Calculated Controls, Controls*

Unbound Object Frame

An unbound object frame is a control that displays objects (graphic objects, video, sounds, and more) that are not stored in a table. An unbound object frame always displays the same object regardless of which record is displayed.

SEE ALSO *Controls*

Underlining see Formatting Controls

Underlying Table or Query

An underlying table or query is the table or query that contains the data you want to display in a form or report.

Undoing Mistakes

If you make a mistake (such as inadvertently moving a well-positioned set of controls out of position), you can undo your action by choosing the Edit→Undo command. If you change your mind and want to undo what you undid, choose the Edit→Redo command.

You can also use the Undo and Redo buttons on the various Design toolbars. By clicking the arrow on the Undo or Redo button, you can undo or redo several recent actions.

Validation Rules

A field's Validation Rule property sets limits or conditions on the data that can be entered in the field. For example, you could require credit card expiration date entries to be later than the current date (so you know that the credit account is valid the day you take the order).

To create a validation rule, you enter an expression in the field's Validation Rule property box. An expression is a combination of symbols and values that produce a specific result because Access understands the expression.

A validation rule can be created for a field in a table, and that validation rule is carried into any object where that field is displayed. It can also be created in a form control for the field, without affecting the underlying field in the table or in any other objects or controls.

There are specific symbols and syntax involved in creating a functional expression, and you need to study them a bit to create a good, custom validation rule expression. But here are a few common expressions you might find useful:

FIELD DATA TYPE	EXPRESSION	DATA LIMITATION
Number, Currency	<>0	No zero values allowed
Number, Currency	0 Or >50	Must be either zero or more than 50
Date/Time	>#1/1/02#	Must be later than January 1, 2002
Date/Time	Between 12/31/01 And 1/1/03	Must be in the year 2002
Date/Time	>Now()	Must be later than the current date and time
Text	Like "P???"	Must be four characters, beginning with **P**

To create a validation rule in a table field, open the table in Design view. Click in the field row, and then type the expression in the Validation Rule box in the Field Properties pane.

To create a validation rule in a form control, open the form in Design view. Right-click the control, and click Properties. On the Data tab, type the expression in the Validation Rule property box.

Validation Text

Validation text is a custom message that's displayed if invalid data is entered in a field or control where a validation rule exists.

To create a validation text message for a table field, open the table in Design view. Click in the field row, and then type the text in the Validation Text box in the Field Properties pane.

To create a validation text message for a form control, open the form in Design view. Right-click the control, and click Properties. On the Data tab, type the text in the Validation Text property box.

Value

A value is the data contained in a single field in a single record. For example, a customer's first name or a record's ID number is the record's value in that field.

Versions, Converting

In all versions of Access, there's no backward compatibility. In other words, you cannot open a database that was saved in a more current version of Access (for example, you cannot open an Access 2000 database in Access 97). When you open an older-version database in a current version of Access (for example, an Access 97 database in Access 2002), you must convert it to the new version to be able to work in it.

What's new in Access 2002 is that you can work in a database created in either Access 2000 or in Access 2002. In fact, the default version that new Access 2002 databases are created in is Access 2000, so that you can use the database in either Access 2000 or Access 2002.

NOTE   *The database version, 2000 or 2002, appears in the title bar of the database window.*

In Access 2002, you can easily convert any database into the 97, 2000, or 2002 file format. To convert a database: open the database, but close any database objects. Choose the Tools→Database Utilities→Convert Database command, and select the version you want. In the Convert Database Into dialog box, you'll be asked to give the database file a new name, because you're actually creating a new database in the different version.

NOTE   *You'll still have the original, unconverted database on your hard drive.*

Before the conversion is complete, you'll see a message with details you need to know about the new version.

Views

Each database object has a Design view and a working view. The working view name depends on the object (Form view for forms, Preview for reports, Datasheet view for tables and queries).

To switch between views for an open object, click the View button on the Access toolbar. You can also click the arrow on the View button and select a view from the list.

Visual Basic

Microsoft builds a programming language, called Visual Basic for Applications, into the Access program. When you create a command button using the Controls Wizard, for example, what Access actually does is write a Visual Basic program to perform the selected actions.

SEE ALSO *Macros*

Windows

Everything in a Windows program is contained in windows on your computer screen, and all windows can be resized, minimized, maximized, and moved around on the screen. A few important items about the specific types of Access windows will help you to work more efficiently in Access.

Access Window

The Access window is the program window in which all the database windows are contained. The Access toolbars and window buttons (Minimize, Restore/Maximize, and Close) are found along the top of the Access window. It's easiest to work in Access if the Access window is maximized.

Database Window

Only one database file can be open at a time, so you'll only see a single database window in the Access program window. The database window is most efficient if it's an intermediate size, so that when you open object windows (for forms, tables, and so forth), you can see all the different windows and switch between them easily.

NOTE   *When you maximize any database or object window, all the database and object windows are maximized. When you Restore any window size, all the database and object windows are restored to an intermediate size.*

Object Windows

Each object, such as a form, report, table, or query, opens in its own object window. You can have many object windows open at the same time. For many database objects, the working view (such as the Form view for a form) is easiest to use in an intermediate size, but when you switch the object to Design view, it's easier to work with the window maximized.

Wizards

Wizards are Access features that help you create databases and database objects by asking you questions and then using your input to create the objects.

Database Wizard

The Database Wizard will create and customize one of the built-in databases for you. To start the Database Wizard: choose the File→New command. In the New File task pane, under New From Template, click General Templates. In the Templates dialog box, on the Databases tab, double-click a database file type, and the wizard starts.

Form Wizard

The Form Wizard will help you create a form from a single table, multiple tables, or a query, and is a good way to start building a form (you let the wizard do the tedious work for you, and then you can customize the form when the wizard is finished). To start the Form Wizard: in the database window, in the Forms group, double-click Create Form By Using Wizard.

Report Wizard

The Report Wizard will help you create a report from a single table, multiple tables, or a query, and is the best way to start building a report. After the Report Wizard does all the basic work, you can customize the report. To start the Report Wizard: in the database window, in the Reports group, double-click Create Report By Using Wizard.

Table Wizard

The Table Wizard is one way to create a new table—not always the best, but it can be a timesaver if there's a pre-built table template that is appropriate for your purposes. To start the Table Wizard: in the database window, in the Tables group, double-click Create Table By Using Wizard.

Controls Wizard

The Controls Wizard helps you build some of the controls for forms and reports. Many controls don't require a wizard, but some (such as the combo box and list box) do need the wizard, and some, such as the command button, will use the wizard to program the control's actions with VBA programming code.

The Controls Wizard is the button in the upper-right corner of the Toolbox (shown in Figure W-1). To use the Controls Wizard: in the Toolbox, make sure the Controls Wizard button is highlighted before you create the control you want. If you don't want to use the Controls Wizard to build a control (for example, if you want an un-programmed command button with which you can run a macro), click the Control Wizard button to turn it off.

Figure W-1   The button in the upper-right corner is the Controls Wizard.

Zoom

The Zoom box, which appears on the toolbar when a report is open in Print Preview, lets you magnify or reduce the size of the report pages that show in the report window. To use the Zoom box, select or enter a percent in the Zoom box.

When a report is open in Print Preview, you can quickly zoom in to full size and out to fit the whole page in the window by clicking the report page with the mouse. In Print Preview, the mouse looks like a magnifying glass, and clicking on the report page switches between zoomed in and zoomed out.

TIP   *You can also show more than one page in the Print Preview window, by clicking the Two Pages or Multiple Pages buttons on the toolbar.*

Zoom Pointer

The zoom pointer is the mouse pointer, which takes the shape of a magnifying glass when you move it over a Report in Print Preview; clicking the zoom pointer magnifies and reduces the Report view.

INDEX

Symbols

A

B

C

G

Access 2002 From A to Z

S

Access 2002 From A to Z